A Case for the Candle Maker

A Case for the Candle Maker

An Ainsley McGregor Mystery

Candace Havens

TULE
PUBLISHING

A Case for the Candle Maker
Copyright© 2021 Candace Havens
Tule Publishing First Printing, February 2021

The Tule Publishing, Inc.

ALL RIGHTS RESERVED

First Publication by Tule Publishing 2021

Cover design by Sue Traynor

No part of this book may be used or reproduced in any manner whatsoever without written permission except in the case of brief quotations embodied in critical articles and reviews.

This is a work of fiction. Names, characters, places, and incidents are products of the author's imagination or are used fictitiously. Any resemblance to actual events, locales, organizations, or persons, living or dead, is entirely coincidental.

ISBN: 978-1-953647-83-2

Dedication

This book is dedicated to the Tule Gang. You have no idea how grateful I am for you all.

Chapter One

BLESS YOUR ART buzzed with people buying Valentine's gifts, which should have made me so happy. Okay, it did. But having three of my crafters, the ones who were supposed to be running the registers, out with the flu was not so fun.

George Clooney sighed at my feet. "I promise, dude, as soon as it dies down we'll go out."

He grunted like he didn't believe me.

"I don't blame you." I'd been saying the same thing for an hour but there hadn't been a lull in the shop since we opened the doors. Valentine's was coming up and people were getting desperate.

I understood. I had no idea what to get Jake, my *boyfriend*. Yep. Still weird to even think that word.

We'd decorated the shop in red and white, and a row of red shiny hearts fell off the far wall, just as I shoved my new bangs out of my face.

They were cute, but constantly in my eyes.

"I don't get it," a woman said. She'd just walked in from the outside, and up to the register.

"Can I help you?"

"Are you Ainsley?"

"Yes." I forced a smile.

"I just don't get it. What a waste." Then she turned and left. She took off down the sidewalk like demons chased her.

"What's a waste?" I had no idea who she was, or what she was talking about.

A line had formed and I turned my attention back to my work.

A woman who reminded me of Halle Berry—like so beautiful she belonged on a magazine cover—cleared her throat.

"Excuse me?" she said softly.

Maybe it was low blood sugar but I had the toughest time focusing.

She put a couple of candles on the counter but I didn't recognize them. A soft scent of vanilla and cinnamon wafted through my sinuses. The tension in my shoulders dropped and I sighed happily. But when I went to look for the code on the bottom, I didn't find one.

"These are beautiful. Unfortunately, they don't have a code on the bottom. Can you tell me what booth you were in when you picked them up?" While I tried to keep the inventory of Bless Your Art in my head, we had a big store. It was possible I'd missed these.

"I made them," she said quickly. "I was wondering if I could sell them in your shop. The one you picked up is the stress relief one. But I have ones for love, others for energy. I heard about your shop from a guy I met last month at a festival. He runs a carnival. I'm embarrassed that I can't remember his name, but he said I should come see you."

I smiled. "Was it Rob?" He was the only guy I knew who owned a carnival. Once I'd figured out he wasn't a deranged killer, we'd become good friends.

The woman snapped her fingers. "Yes. He said to tell you that my sleep candle works."

While I was always looking for new vendors, there wasn't a lot of space in the shop at the moment.

"Do you mind if we do the first batch on consignment?" That was a much safer bet financially. While the shop was in the black, it wasn't always easy to keep it that way.

"I don't mind at all. And I won't need much space. I'll give you several to burn. The orange blossom one is great for shoppers. The smell energizes them."

Each candle was decorated with tiny gold stars, moons, or beads. They were burning works of art. They had a small card that said what the aroma might help with, from love to prosperity to sleep.

Candles with a story. I loved it. I was always on the lookout for something new and different.

I glanced around the shop. There was a round display table with a collection of things from the shop that was nearly empty. And if I moved some things on the shelf above it, it would work perfectly.

"What smells so good?" a shopper said behind the woman who'd brought the candles.

"Her candles," I said. That's when I realized I hadn't introduced myself.

"I'm Ainsley McGregor," I said with a little wave.

"I'm Jasmine Levy," she said, and then smiled. "I know you're busy—if you show me where you want me to set up, I can do it myself. I don't want to keep your customers waiting."

I pointed toward the round table and the shelves. "I was thinking there would be nice."

Jasmine glanced back. "That's perfect. Are you sure? That's prime real estate for a shop like this."

"Of, course. Mrs. Whedon? Could you find a box for the items left on the table? So, we can clear the space?"

The octogenarian, who was dressed in an avocado jumpsuit, looked up from her knitting, but the needles didn't stop moving. Her booth was in the front row of the store.

"Yes," she said in her clipped manor. And then hopped up like a twenty-year-old and fast-walked to the back of the store.

"Oh, we didn't need to bug her." Jasmine frowned. "I have some boxes out in my car."

"It's okay. She loves to be needed," I whispered. "And if she's gruff with you, that means she likes you."

Jasmine smiled. "My gran used to be that way."

"You go on over and start setting up. When I finish with the customers in line, I'll help you."

Her smile was wide. "Thank you so much." She picked up a box on the floor, but then turned back. She put it down, and then pulled a box of matches from her pocket. "Why don't I light an orange one for you."

She did so, and then picked up the box again. As she walked past the customers, they turned and followed her.

"What other smells do you have?" the woman who had been behind Jasmine asked. As she explained what each candle did, Mrs. Whedon returned.

As Jasmine took the candles out of the box, people were

grabbing them out of her hands. I pulled a sheet of inventory stickers from the stack under the counter, and headed to the table. While I tried to put them on the bottom of the candles, people were buying more and more.

"Is that all you have?" one woman asked.

Jasmine shook her head. "I have a lot more in my car. Just give me a second."

"Mrs. Whedon, would you be able to check them out so I can help Jasmine?"

"Ainsley McGregor, I'm not some feeble old woman," she said.

I bit my lip to keep from smiling. She was as grumpy as they came but she had a heart of fluffy marshmallows. "Yes, ma'am." She had more energy than I did most days, so who was I to argue.

I followed Jasmine out to her SUV. It was packed with boxes. When she opened the hatch on the back, a cacophony of smells erupted.

It was glorious.

"At the rate your candles are selling, you may go through all of this inventory in a day."

She laughed. "No one is more surprised than I am how well these sell. This same sort of thing has been happening to me at the festivals. I'm grateful, but surprised."

She peeked inside the boxes. "That box just behind this one is the love candles."

Love candles. It just sounded funny.

"So, how did you get into candle making? Have you always done it?"

She laughed. "No. I was—I—consulted with high-powered businesses and helped them restructure. But after ten years, it was wearing on me. I retired. I just couldn't do it anymore."

"You're so young to have retired."

"I guess I shouldn't say retire, because the candles have become a full-time business, but I love it. I found this old recipe book in my grandmother's trunk. It had been locked for thirty years. I watched a video on how to pick locks and I was able to open it."

That's how I'd learned most of what I knew about being an amateur detective. YouTube and detective shows were responsible for my knowledge base.

"That was smart—about the video," I said. "I'm surprised no one tried to cut the lock."

She smiled. "Oh, it was a thing with my mom. She said whatever was in there was best hidden away. I remember her being a little wary of my dad's mom. I don't know what made me decide to open it that day, but I did.

"Several old books were in there. She had recipes for everything from healing aids, to how to get rid of pests, to love potions. But I was drawn to the candle-making ones. There was a recipe for soothing the soul. It's eucalyptus mixed with vanilla and some other things. That first batch of candles were lopsided. But when I burned them, I felt better."

She shook her head. "Sorry. I love my candles. Can you tell?"

"Oh, don't be sorry. I think it's fascinating. Almost like your grandmother guided you to do all of that."

She sat the box she'd been holding back down, and then put her hand on my arm. "You and I are going to be fast friends, Ainsley McGregor. I very much like how you think. And I'm so grateful to you for taking on my candles."

"I'm happy you walked into my store. And you're right. You have a lot in common with me and my friend Shannon. She owns the coffee shop on the corner. We were both doing other things before starting our own businesses."

Three women came out of the store, and all of them were talking about the candles.

"I think it's me, who should be thanking you," I said. "Since you're new in town, why don't you meet me and my friend Shannon for dinner. We're going to Dooley's at the corner around seven."

"Oh, I wouldn't want to impose."

"You won't be. She's getting married in three weeks and always needs a distraction these days."

"Well, it would be nice to have company for dinner."

We picked up the boxes again, and headed into the store.

I was looking forward to learning more about the beautiful Jasmine.

AS EXPECTED, JASMINE and Shannon quickly became friends at dinner. Helped by the fact that the other woman asked her about every detail of the wedding—which, rightfully so, was Shannon's favorite topic these days.

As maid of honor, I'd been involved in every aspect of planning the nuptials, but I still loved that my friend was so excited about marrying one of the best guys, Mike, that I'd ever met. He owned the local winery, and had a booth in my store.

"I'm bringing out four desserts for you guys," Dooley said. It was his restaurant. He had the appearance of a scary biker dude with an aversion to shirts with sleeves. But he was kind and one heck of a chef.

"Four?" Jasmine asked.

"Dooley understands that Shannon and I are dessert connoisseurs and we never mind helping him try out new recipes."

Everyone laughed.

"So, let me guess, we're doing a tasting for your Valentine's dinner? What are you bringing us?" Shannon asked.

Dooley pointed his finger toward her. "Got it in one. And I've got a cherry tart, blueberry love cake, strawberry cheesecake topped with ganache, and chocolate-covered strawberry brownies."

"Um. Yum."

He headed back to the kitchen.

Jasmine glanced around the restaurant. "I really like this town. Everyone is so kind. It's different than I remember it."

"You've been here before?" I asked.

"My grandmother used to live here. She owned the mill, and a couple of other businesses. I think she was even mayor once. It was a big deal because it was before the civil rights movement. And she was a black woman in a small town in Texas."

"Ms. Johnson?" Shannon asked. "Oh my goodness. You're like Sweet River royalty."

Jasmine laughed.

"Ains, your building used to be the old Johnson mill."

"Oh. Wow. I had no idea."

"I think it closed before I was born," Jasmine said. "You know, it's funny. I remembered having family in this area, but now I know why I was drawn here. Strange how that happens."

"Does your family still own land around here?" I asked.

"It's a possibility. My mom's side of the family owned some property here, and my dad wasn't fond of them. At least, that's what I remember. She died when we were pretty young."

"I'm sorry for your loss," I said.

"Thanks. It still hurts and it's been twenty years."

"We should do some research on your family while you're here. I bet the courthouse would have records of all the land deeds. I'll help if you like. I love doing research."

"She loves snooping," Shannon said with a smile. "And she's really good at it. I'll help, too."

"So, is everyone in this town as kind as you two?"

We laughed.

Shannon nodded. "Sweet River has that name for a reason. The people here are kind. For the most part, it's almost perfect. I mean, everyone knows each other and looks out for their neighbors. But then they all know your business, as well."

"There is that," I said. "It's impossible to keep a secret around here."

"Right?" Shannon laughed. "Sometimes it feels like they know your business before you do."

Jasmine smiled but it didn't quite reach her eyes. "I've been living in Houston the last year. I don't even know what my neighbors in my condo building look like. It can feel really isolating sometimes." Her voice grew soft. She waved a hand, as if pushing the bad memories away. "But at least no one knows that I just bought four boxes of Little Debbie's oatmeal cookies."

"The ones with the creamy stuff in the center?" I asked.

She nodded.

"Those are like crack for me," I said. "A few months ago, I accused my poor dog, George, of eating them. But all the wrappers were in the trash can, which means it was me. I ate the whole box in one night."

At that moment, Dooley placed a huge tray of desserts—way more than four—on our table. "Enjoy. And let me know which ones you prefer."

We all laughed.

"Goodness, I don't know when I've laughed so much," Jasmine said. "Maybe, I'm a little too used to being alone."

"Well, you've got us now," Shannon said. "Friends for life. Ainsley and I are pretty hard to shake."

"You sound like a stalker," I said. "But she's right. You are our kind of people."

"I feel the same way about you two. I'm so lucky that I walked into your store," Jasmine said.

"Me, too. And I swear it has nothing to do with the fact that we sold out of your candles in just a few hours."

Jasmine shook her head. "I still can't believe it. I'll bring you some more in the morning."

"Excellent," I said. "Now what dessert are we trying first?"

I was surprised we didn't need a wheelbarrow to roll us

out of Dooley's by the time we were finished. My eyes were already drooping with the need for an extreme food nap.

Luckily, the wind had picked up and the temperature had dropped to about fifty. It seldom was below seventy here in the winter, but every once in a while a cold front pushed through.

"Would you like me to drive you down to the B&B?" I asked.

Shannon pulled on a puffy jacket, which had been tied around her waist.

"Oh. No. I'll be fine. It's only two blocks, and after that meal, I need to walk. You two go on."

She put on her dark green coat. With her knee-high black boots, she could have been doing a winter photo shoot. She was that beautiful.

"If you're sure. We don't mind," Shannon added. I was taking her out to Mike's winery, where George was. Her fiancé had been kind enough to dog-sit for me during our girls' night.

"I promise, I'm good. I love to walk."

We said our goodbyes, and then Shannon and I started toward my car.

Something made me shiver that had nothing to do with the cold. I stopped and turned around.

I could barely make out her form but Jasmine paused. I swear it looked like she was arguing with a bush.

"What's wrong?" Shannon asked. She must have realized I wasn't beside her and had come back to my spot.

"I had one of my feelings," I said.

"About Jasmine?"

I shook my head. "I don't know."

"Let's drive down the block," Shannon said, anxiously.

We hurried to my car.

But by the time we drove down toward the B&B, Jasmine was nowhere to be seen.

"She's probably a fast walker," Shannon said. "But I can go into the B&B and check."

"I'm sure she's fine," I said. "Besides, it's after nine and you know the door is locked. If you wake up Mrs. Carmichael—"

"Yeah. No," Shannon said. We both laughed. "That woman is protective of her guests and her beauty sleep." We'd learned that the hard way.

"Oh. Look. There she is."

A light on the second floor had popped on, and Jasmine's silhouette was on the curtains.

"Okay. Good. I just wanted to make sure she was all right."

The businesses of Sweet River, with the exception of Dooley's, and a couple of other restaurants and bars, were all closed by seven.

So, who in the world had she been talking to this late at night?

Chapter Two

THE NEXT MORNING George and I were a little late getting to the shop. It had a bit to do with the sugar coma I'd been in by the time I'd made it home last night. I'd changed quickly and fell into bed—and forgot to set my alarm.

Then there was the fact that I'd run out of coffee at home. I'm not even sure how that happened. No one can talk to me before I've had a cup.

Luckily, after texting my plight to Shannon, she ran some coffee and bagels out to the car for me, so George didn't have to sit outside while I ran in for some.

I rolled down the window. "Thank you, Coffee Goddess."

"You are welcome. And I put a treat in for you, George."

He barked.

"I swear he understands every word we say," Shannon said.

"Or he knows the word treat."

He barked again. We laughed.

I'd pulled into my spot behind the shop. After taking three quick sips of coffee, I turned to George. "Whew. I needed that."

"Ruh-huh," he said. And then licked my ear with his giant tongue.

"Gross. Dude. You have to stop doing that. And I promise, I'll give you the treat she put in the bag when we get inside."

He whined as if he were in a hurry to get out of the car. I hadn't lied to Shannon. My dog understood anything that had to do with food.

I shouldn't have worried about being late. Mrs. Whedon, Don—who is our resident Santa—and Mike were busy replenishing the shelves of the various booths, and sweeping.

"You guys are awesome!" I yelled out.

"Darn straight," Mrs. Whedon said. "Where have you been?" The words came out way sharper than I'm sure she meant.

"Forgot to set my alarm." After putting my things in the office, I put on a Bless Your Art apron, and grabbed the cleaner to wipe down the front counter.

"Is the candle lady coming today?" Don asked. "Peggy heard about them through the grapevine, and I've been ordered to pick up one of each kind."

I laughed. "Maybe we should all go into the candle-making business. But yes, she's supposed to bring us more this morning."

We all set about making the shop sparkly for our customers. By the time we opened, there were people waiting at the door. Most of whom went straight for the table with the candles.

They smelled really good. I'd lit the one on the front counter. But I didn't understand the big draw—I mean, I was grateful, but they were just candles.

"I need more of the love candle," a woman said as she headed to the front counter. "There aren't any left. I need it for tonight. I have a date."

"Oh. I guess we must be out of that one."

She waved a hand in my face. "Well, don't you have some more in the back?"

"No," I said.

Her eyebrow went up. "Well, when will you have some more? My friend told me that she used it and her husband said they should go to Paris for their anniversary. That he'd never been so romantic."

What can I say? People are weird. There's no way a candle compelled some guy to do that. "I'll call the woman who makes them. Why don't you look around the shop."

She harrumphed but walked away.

I called Jasmine but she didn't answer. I left a message.

Half of the customers who had walked into the store had been asking for her candles. And Jasmine hadn't been returning my calls.

I hadn't known her long, but something didn't feel right. She seemed like more a type A person than a flake. I was worried something might have happened.

Maria had come in and I decided to take a break and walk George.

The weather was cold, so I grabbed my jacket and the leash.

A few minutes later we'd walked the two blocks across the park to the back of the B&B. Mrs. Carmichael was out there wrapping her precious rose bushes in burlap.

"Do you need help?" I asked. But she didn't answer or

even acknowledge I was there.

"Mrs. Carmichael?"

I walked up and touched her shoulder. She let out an ear-splitting scream. And stabbed out with the scissors she'd been using to cut the burlap. Lucky for me, George yanked me back just in time. Then proceeded to let Mrs. Carmichael have it. He barked viciously at her.

"George. No." He stopped immediately, but he growled under his breath. He was not a happy dog.

"Oh, dear," the older woman said loudly. She threw the shears to the ground, and then fumbled with something in her pocket. "I had my hearing aid turned down again and I didn't realize it. I could have killed you. And poor George, I gave him a fright."

"It's okay," I said. Though, my hands still shook and I was fairly certain it wasn't from the cold. She was right. If George hadn't pulled me out of the way—it could have been scary.

"No. It isn't. I know better. Why don't you two come inside. I just put out the lunch. I've got some of my peanut butter cookies for dessert and we know George loves those."

My dog may have grabbed an entire tray of said cookies at the church bake sale a few weeks ago.

"Oh, it's okay. I just came by to check on Jasmine. She isn't answering her phone."

"Jasmine? Oh, the Peony Room. I'm old, and terrible with names. I remember our guests by the rooms they stay in. Come to think of it, I haven't seen her today. She didn't come down for breakfast. Come on inside and warm up."

George and I followed her through the back into the

kitchen. "You two have a seat and I'll ring her room."

The old Victorian had been fitted with a huge, modern kitchen. The rest of the B&B was true to the time the house was built. But the kitchen was white marble counters and white cabinets and lots of windows letting the sun in. She walked quickly into the hallway, and then came back with a couple of cookies.

"You two snack on these. Consider it my peace offering for you not calling your brother with assault charges. I'll be right back."

She left again and was gone for a while. George had taken care of both of our cookies, without me realizing it.

"Ainsley, I need your help."

I followed her voice to the front parlor stairs.

"What's wrong?"

"Well, she didn't answer. And I just checked with Karen Ann, who tried to clean the room this morning and it was locked from the inside. I just tried again and it is still locked from the inside. I can't get my master key to work."

I wasn't sure what she expected me to do. But before I could make it two steps up, George bounded past me.

"George! Get back down here." It was one thing for him to be at the back of the house. Quite another for him to be out front where her guests were.

"I'm so sorry," I said, as I rushed past her.

But then he started that low menacing growl. The one that had the pit of my stomach twisting into knots.

"What's wrong with him?" Mrs. Carmichael sounded more worried than disturbed.

"Could be anything from a squirrel to the heater. He's

not a friend of either." I didn't want to frighten her. And it was true. Squirrels were the bane of his existence. And he treated the heated floor vents in my house like little kids do the game Lava. Anytime they were blowing out warm air, he carefully navigated around them.

By the time I made it upstairs, the growl had turned into a weird whine. I'd heard it before and it was never good news.

Dear, God. Please let Jasmine be okay. My mouth turned to cotton and the knot in my stomach tightened.

I tried the door but to no avail.

"Maybe, you should call that handsome boyfriend of yours," she said.

Jake was a fireman and today he was training his men on new emergency procedures. He and I were in a good place, even though we were two ships passing in the day—he'd been working nights, lately. We had completely opposite schedules.

"He and the guys are super busy today. Besides, I don't think you want them chopping through your beautiful mahogany door."

"You are right about that, dear."

"Do you by chance have a ladder? Maybe she left and the door jammed when she closed it. I have that problem with the old doors at my house. Before we call emergency services, let me make sure she's in the room." Though, if she were, there was no way she'd be able to sleep through the commotion George made.

"I've got one," she said.

A few minutes later, I put the ladder up against the outside wall.

This was definitely more Jake's thing than mine. I'm not super crazy about heights. My worry for Jasmine, though, outweighed the fear.

"I'll hold it. You climb up."

I didn't think she'd be strong enough to keep me from falling, but the longer I waited, the more my nerves jangled through my body.

Luckily, I didn't have to climb all the way to the top to reach the second-floor window.

The room was dark, and the sky cloudy. At first, I couldn't see much. And then the sun broke through and cast some light on the bed. A figure lay there, curled into a ball. I banged on the window so hard I worried I might break it. "Jasmine? It's Ainsley. From the shop? Hello?"

But the figure didn't move.

George's whines persisted at the base of the ladder.

As much as I didn't want to admit it—something was very wrong with my new friend.

I shoved upward on the window, but it didn't budge.

My throat was dry and tears burned. I'd just met Jasmine, but I'd really liked her. She hadn't seemed ill at all. In fact, she was the picture of health.

The sun broke through the clouds a bit more. Her back was toward the window but I watched her for several minutes. She never took a breath.

"Mrs. Carmichael?"

"Is everything, okay?"

"No, ma'am. You'd better call my brother."

Chapter Three

SINCE THE STATION, which was a part of city hall, was across the street from the B&B, Greg and his men were there soon after I made it down the ladder. While some of his men were out of breath, my brother was not. He was a health nut, even more so since Lucy, who was a detective, had moved into his house.

I had a feeling they were dating, but he kept saying they were just good friends. I wasn't so sure Lucy felt the same way—since she had an obvious crush on my brother.

"What's going on?" He followed us into the B&B. "And why were you on a ladder?"

"My friend is in a room that is locked from the inside," I said. I leaned in. "Something is wrong. I think she might be dead," I whispered.

"And you know her?"

"I just met her yesterday but Shannon and I had dinner with her last night. You know how you meet someone and you feel like you've known them forever? That's the way it was for all of us. I really liked her."

My voice caught at the end. It wasn't like me to cry or be overly emotional. Greg frowned.

He ran up the steps and tried the door.

"Do you want me to get the axe?" Kevin, who usually

worked the front desk at the station, asked.

"No," we all chimed in at the same time. Mrs. Carmichael may have been the loudest.

"Those doors are more than 150 years old," she said. "I've got a hammer and a long nail so you can pop it off the hinges. We had to do that several years ago, when I opened the B&B."

A short time later, they had the door off. It was crowded up there, so I waited on the downstairs landing with Mrs. Carmichael.

When Greg came out of the room, he had his phone in his hand. He motioned for his guys to cordon off the space.

Then, he headed downstairs.

I started to ask a question, but his phone rang.

"Yep. We're at the B&B. How soon can you get here? Okay, I'll have my guys wait. Thanks, Kane."

Kane was the medical examiner and coroner for several counties.

That meant my instinct was right.

Mrs. Carmichael's hand shook in mine. "Oh. My. That poor woman. She was so sweet," she said.

"Why don't we go sit down," I said.

"I just—she was so young," she said. Just as we passed the front door, it opened.

Mrs. Carmichael and I gasped in unison.

There stood Jasmine holding a box of candles.

Chapter Four

My brother Greg rounded us all up and put us in the lounge at the back of the B&B. The forensic team was still upstairs. George was by the fire, and snored softly for once.

Jasmine was in the corner of a big sectional, dabbing her nose with a tissue. Mrs. Carmichael had been kind enough to make some coffee and put out some Valentine's cookies.

I was in a soft cushy chair, and if I hadn't just had the shock of my life, I might have been able to have a nap. As it was, I very much needed to know who was in Jasmine's room.

"We can do this later," Greg said. "But if you can just give me a name so I can let the coroner know who she is, that will help us a great deal."

Jasmine gave a long shuddering sigh.

"I just needed a minute," she said. She pulled her knees up to her chest. After taking a long breath, she shook her head.

"It's my sister," she said. "Her name is Nia Levy."

Tears rolled down her cheeks.

"We—I've—oh this is just a mess." Jasmine blew her nose. "Let me gather my thoughts."

Greg, being the good cop he was, didn't push. He just

sat and waited as she composed herself. I was just as anxious.

Kane hadn't arrived yet to tell us how the woman died, but it was a strange situation. I happen to know my brother believes strange and suspicious usually go together. But how could anyone hurt someone who was in a locked room?

Not that anyone had mentioned murder. But every time George gave that weird whine of his, it almost always ended up being exactly that.

I didn't think Jasmine murdered someone and left them in her room. Greg hadn't said anything but I knew my brother. The obvious suspect in all of this would be the only person in town who knew the victim. Jasmine didn't seem like a killer, but I never assumed anything anymore.

"Goodness. I can't believe she's dead," Jasmine said softly. "I haven't seen her in maybe ten years. I tried to keep up through social media, but my family isn't big about airing their lives online." Jasmine wrung her hands. "I can't believe—I don't understand why she's gone. We just found each other again."

Grief sat heavy on her shoulders as she shook her head. "Last night, when she approached me on the street, I didn't recognize her at first. I have no idea how she found me. It's all so—I don't know. Weird."

"Can you explain why you and your family were estranged?" Greg asked.

I wanted to high-five my brother. That was exactly what I would have asked, but I was worried it might make Jasmine look more guilty.

"My dad didn't like my politics or my outspoken nature." Jasmine pursed her lips. "When I turned seventeen, I went to college and never went back home. He was determined to get me under his thumb, and none of this will help you. Basically, if my sisters tried to contact me, they were out of the will.

"And there's a lot of money involved. It was tough for a long time, but I had to move on. It was not a healthy household. A year and a half ago, I had a health scare and contacted my sisters to let them know."

She chewed on her lip. "My dad found out that I'd contacted them. His lawyers sent me a letter and I expected the worst. But the note was from my dad. He gave me his number and asked if, when I was ready, I'd call him."

Wow, that was quite a story.

"My head hurts," she said. She pinched the skin above her nose.

I jumped up. "Mrs. Carmichael, do you have some aspirin or ibuprofen?" The B&B owner had been sitting in the dining room, no doubt listening to every word.

"Yes, of course," she said.

"We can take a break," Greg offered. "If you want to come to the station later."

Jasmine shook her head. "I'll tell you whatever you want to know. Please, you have to find out what happened to Nia. She was the smartest of all of us. I keep saying this—but I can't believe she's gone."

Mrs. Carmichael handed her a glass of water and a bottle of pills. Jasmine took a couple.

"Did you have a chance to talk to your father?"

She nodded. "He said he was sorry about everything. That he'd misjudged me. Turns out, my warning to my sisters saved their lives. I had ovarian cancer. My doctors caught it early enough, but I wanted my sisters to get tested."

When she'd said health scare, I thought mono or something. Cancer was a big deal and she looked amazing. It was hard to believe she'd been sick.

"Anyway, it had been so long since I'd heard his voice, that I wasn't sure it was really him. He was ready to retire from the company, and he wanted me to think about coming home to run it with my sisters. He'd heard about my success in the business world. He was proud of me."

She sobbed, and then waved her hand. "I'm so sorry. It's all—this is a lot."

"When was it that you first spoke to your dad?"

"About six months ago?"

"And did you take him up on the offer?" Greg asked.

"I told him that I'd think about it. But that I too was retiring to do what I loved. He asked me to come home this summer for a visit and said that he needed to put things right. We had a lot of bad blood between us. I told him I'd think about it."

Greg shifted in his seat. "Did your sister, Nia, tell you why she was here?"

Jasmine bit her lip. "They've been trying to get in touch with me, but in these small towns my cell never works. Nia said she tracked me down to tell me that Dad had passed away a few days ago. It was the only thing she said that made sense. I don't know if she was drunk, or so upset that she wasn't thinking clearly, but she kept saying weird things. Like, she didn't know what to do about Dad. That I'd have to take care of things. That it was too late.

"But when I tried to pin her down and figure out what she was talking about, she'd just start crying."

Tears streamed down her face. "He was a mean old goat, but he was my dad." She sobbed again. "I just don't understand any of this. Do they know how Nia died? My poor sister. She was always the rock and if Dad is gone…"

Two family deaths in just a few days? This did not look good.

Lucy came to doorway of the parlor and nodded toward Greg.

"Excuse me for just a minute." He turned off his phone, which he'd been using in addition to a pen and paper to write down notes.

I went over to the couch and hugged Jasmine. "I'm so sorry for your loss…losses," I corrected. "I can't even imagine what you are going through."

She hugged me tight. "Thank you for staying here with me. Everything is so…surreal. Like, I'm in the middle of a terrible nightmare, and I'll wake up any minute.

"I should call my sisters. They need to know. Oh. This all so awful."

"It is. My guess is the police have already let them know. They are good about that."

Kane passed Greg and Lucy. He listened to what Greg had to say. He frowned, and glanced into the room where we sat. I was glad Jasmine's head was down.

Kane headed upstairs, and then Greg sat down in the chair where I'd been.

He smiled at Jasmine. "Miss Levy, do you feel like continuing?"

"Please, call me Jasmine. You can ask me whatever you need."

"So, your sister met you on the street, and you brought her to your room?"

Jasmine blew out a breath. "Nia was freezing. We came inside, and then stood by the fire." She pointed toward the fireplace behind Greg.

"She wasn't making much sense. I understood what she said about Dad, but I wasn't sure I believed her."

"Why is that?"

"Her behavior, it was so odd. You have to understand, I haven't seen her since we were teenagers. And she was two years younger than me. I barely recognized her. She kept saying she was dumb because she didn't figure it out earlier. That I was the only one she could trust. And then it was a lot of gibberish."

She sighed and rubbed her head again. "We were in here for maybe a half hour, and then she was tired. I gave Nia the key and told her to stay in my room. I'll be honest, I needed to be alone for a bit. But when I went upstairs, she'd locked the door. I didn't want to wake anyone up, so I came back down."

She started crying again. "If only I'd banged on that door. She might still be alive." She bit her lip again, and then blew her nose.

"What happened when you couldn't get in?"

"I tried to sleep on the couch here." She patted the sofa. "But I was so wired. My condo is only about an hour and fifteen minutes from here. I needed to make some more candles for Ainsley's store.

"And that kind of work helps soothe my mind. I also have awesome internet and wanted to find out what happened to Dad. But there wasn't a single story. I thought maybe…Nia had gone crazy or something. By then, it was after midnight and I couldn't call anyone in the family. So, I made candles for hours, until I passed out."

She turned toward me. "That's why I was so late getting back this morning. I didn't mean to sleep in."

"Don't worry about it." I hugged her.

"Is there anyone who can verify that you were home?" Greg asked.

She nodded. "I'll be on the security tapes for the building. And the doorman helped me bring stuff in and take stuff out. His name is Bernard."

Greg said, "Okay. I know you might want to go home to your family for your dad's funeral, but it's going to be a few days before we can release your sister's body."

Jasmine covered her face with her hands. "I don't even know how all that works and I need to contact my family. To lose Dad and Nia so close together—"

"We should have cause of death in the next forty-eight hours or so. We can contact your family—we actually need to talk to them." Greg closed his notebook.

She'd just lost her dad, who sounded like he'd wanted to make amends, and her sister, who she'd only just been reunited with. If anything, this was the time she'd need her family the most.

"I—Oh, okay. But I'd really like the news about Jasmine to come from me." She frowned. "Actually, they'll just blame me. Say I did something. You can call them. Just let them know I'll be bringing her back as soon as possible."

Mrs. Carmichael offered Jasmine a different room so she could rest, and the poor woman took her up on it. So many thoughts were whirring through my brain. Everything about Jasmine and her family was like a made-for-TV movie.

Greg stood and stretched. "Don't you need to get back to the store?"

I frowned. I did. They probably thought I fell into a hole somewhere.

"What do you think happened to her sister?" I whispered, but it didn't keep my brother from giving me the look. The one that meant I should mind my own business.

"It's too soon to tell and you know that better than most. And I will not be commenting on an ongoing investigation. You just met her yesterday. There is no reason for you to be involved. Okay?"

There was that look again.

"Fine. I just have one thing you might want to think about."

Greg sighed heavily. "What?"

"If it is a suspicious death, what if Nia wasn't the intended target? Jasmine might be in danger."

Chapter Five

GREG WASN'T HAPPY with me. I think more that it didn't occur to him that someone might be trying to kill Jasmine and he was mad that I thought of it first.

"We don't know that it was murder," he said.

"But you had suspicions. Why?"

"The whites of her eyes were a strange color, and her lips had something on them. We'll know more when Kane gets me his report."

"But until then, you'll make sure Jasmine is okay?"

He rolled his eyes.

"I'll leave someone here to keep an eye on her."

BY THE TIME I made it back to the store, we only had a few hours left in the day. It had become gloomy outside, which fit my mood. I do not like finding dead bodies. And if I were honest, I was sad for Jasmine. She had just reconciled with her family, and now some of them were dead.

I came in through the back door. George shivered.

"Tell us everything," Shannon said. She was helping Mike stock wine in his booth.

"Shouldn't you be at work?" I asked the question and

then instantly regretted it. I held up my hands in surrender. "I did not mean it that way."

My friend laughed. "We closed early. Did you not hear about the weather?"

"I've been a bit preoccupied."

She and Mike looked at one another. "We heard."

Of course, they did. This was Sweet River, Texas, after all. It might not be the gossip capital of the world, but it had to be a close runner-up.

"I'll tell you everything but I need to get George a treat. He's been a proper gentleman the last few hours." I headed around the corner to my office where I kept a small container of his favorite treats. He seemed surprised and then gave me that lopsided Great Dane smile that always made me laugh.

"Whew. I needed that, George."

I put the treats, and a fair-sized chewy bone in front of where he lay. "That should keep you busy."

A few minutes later, I was back at Mike's booth. "What's going on with the weather?"

"Ice storm is coming," he said. "Even though it usually doesn't stick here, the temperature has dropped so much that it could."

"I closed the shop early," Shannon said. "I didn't want my employees to have to drive on ice after dark."

I glanced around. We had a few people checking out at the front, but for the most part, the place was empty. "We should do the same. I'll go help up front so we can get people out and lock the door."

"But—" Shannon stared at me expectantly.

"I promise if you give me a call tonight, I'll tell you what I know, which isn't very much."

I pulled my hair into a ponytail and headed up front. George wasn't far behind me with his dog chew in his mouth.

"Is everything okay?" Carrie asked.

"I thought you had band this afternoon?" She was Maria's sixteen-year-old, who was more mature than the rest of us put together. As in, I had no problem leaving my store in her capable hands. She loved it as much as I did.

"Everything with school was canceled, including classes tomorrow." She frowned.

"Only you would be upset about that." I laughed.

She shrugged. "We were going to talk about *Romeo and Juliet* in English today. It's so tragic, and still so relatable."

While she had a big interest in all things to do with boys, she hadn't actually ever dated or fallen for someone. She told me once, that she'd know when she found him. And I agreed with her. I had not been looking for Jake, when he popped up on my doorstep. And now—well, we were getting very cozy. I kind of loved it.

"Shakespeare will still be there when you get back. I don't want you to have to ride your bike home. Mike said the weather will hit pretty fast."

"It's okay. My dad is already out front. I did a last call a few minutes ago for the customers, since I figured you'd want to get home before dark."

Once again, she read my mind. She was uncanny that way. "Good plan and thanks for taking the initiative."

"It's all good. When stuff like this come up, I just put on

my What Would Ainsley Do? hat."

I couldn't help but laugh.

After the last of the customers was out the door, Carrie ran to her dad's car.

Mike was using the big broom to sweep.

"You go home with Shannon. I'll finish this up. It's the least I can do, considering I was gone for so long today."

He shook his head. "Don't worry, really. I'll get everything ready. We're staying at Shannon's tonight so she can open the store tomorrow without traveling on the ice."

"Where did she go?"

"She decided to pack up some food for you and Jake. She said drive to the front door and honk twice, and she'll bring it out."

"She didn't have to do that." Though, I was the last person to turn down food from my friend. She was an amazing cook and baker.

"Have you met my soon-to-be wife? Besides, there's no way we could eat all the leftovers by ourselves."

True. In the South, we like to feed people. It's how we show our love and Shannon was all about that. She and Mike were some of the kindest and most generous people I'd ever met. They were always making meals for the less fortunate or, when there was a disaster, the rescue workers.

They, and so many like them, were the reason I moved to Sweet River. As much as I liked to give the gossips a hard time, people looked out for one another here. And, in general, people were kind.

"Okay. I'll see you—oh, well, depending on the weather, maybe tomorrow?"

He shrugged. "Might be best, even though we've been busy, to keep the store closed—at least until the ice melts."

I nodded. He was right. If someone was hurt trying to get the store, I'd never forgive myself.

A few minutes later, with George sitting in the back seat, I pulled up in front of the coffee shop. I didn't have to honk, Shannon was waiting just inside the front door. She ran out and jumped in my passenger seat. She held up a finger, and then tapped her smart watch. "Okay, you have two minutes to tell me everything."

She was just as nosy as I was about things, and had turned out to be a true partner in crime—well, in solving them.

I told her everything and still had thirty seconds to spare.

"So, what do you think happened?" She wrapped her scarf tighter around her neck. "I don't like that we might have a killer in our midst again."

I shrugged. "I'm more worried about Jasmine. Greg sees her at the top of the suspect list, but I think she might have actually been the target. Of course, I have no proof of any of it. And I shouldn't be making assumptions. She might have died of natural causes. I just have that weird feeling I get, when things aren't right."

"Tell me what I can do to help."

I laughed. "I totally promised Greg that I'd stay out of this. I barely know Jasmine."

She made a raspberry sound.

"That's attractive."

"Since when do you listen to your brother? And I don't know about you, but we had an instant connection with her.

It's like we've known her a long time."

I nodded. "I feel the same way. It's weird. We had one meal with her."

"That's how it is sometimes. I knew you and I would be best friends the first time you came into the coffee shop a few years ago."

I smiled. "You knew exactly what a dirty chai was; it was kismet."

We high-fived. "So, we both feel that way about Jasmine, like she fits right in the friendship circle, and we do anything for our besties. And from the sound of it, she might need someone in her corner."

She was right. More than once I'd put my neck on the line, and other body parts, to help my friends.

"Well, there's not much we can do but research her and the family. You take her dad. She mentioned there was a lot of money involved. And I'll look into her a bit more."

My brother didn't know it, but I still had my password to get into the police records. Or maybe he did, and figured at least I'd have the facts if I started snooping.

He couldn't expect me to do nothing.

"You need to get home. We have our assignments; let's chat later."

She started to get out, and I grabbed her arm gently. "Don't you have a wedding to plan?"

She rolled her eyes. "Ainsley McGregor, I've had my wedding planned since I met Mike four years ago. We have a few last-minute things to pick out, but all of that can be done later in the week. Let's get to sleuthing. We have to help Jasmine."

A WHILE LATER, I pulled in to my drive and stopped to get the mail from the box. Just then, a light went on in my house.

"Who is in the house, George?"

The smart thing to do would be to call my brother. So I did, and of course, he didn't pick up.

I was about to shut the car door, when George bounded out and ran to the front door as if his life depended on it. He was howling like crazy and there was no way I would leave him there.

I texted my brother our special code for when I'm in real trouble. Since I texted him a lot, and often found myself in some kind of trouble, he wanted a way to know if it was a drop everything kind of moment or it could wait.

I sent: *George ate cheese.*

Anyone who knows my dog understands why he must always stay away from cheese. It isn't pretty and is always cause for alarm.

Then, I marched onto the porch to get my dog.

I'd do anything for George, even if it meant risking my life.

Chapter Six

THE WIND PICKED up, and whooshed around the porch and I wished I'd thrown my sweater on before trying to save my dog. "George, hush. Now, the intruder knows we're here. Come on."

My hands shook so hard, I could barely grab ahold of his collar. I tugged, but he didn't move. That's the problem with having a dog that outweighs me by about ten pounds.

"I'm trying to save your life," I whispered, like that would make him understand.

Heavy footsteps clomped on my wooden floors.

"George, please," I begged him but the stubborn dog would not move.

"Ahhhhhhhh," I screamed.

Jake jumped out onto the porch with his fists up. "What's wrong? Did someone hurt you?"

He glanced around looking for danger. In his defense, that's happened more than once for me—someone trying to kill me at my house.

With my heart in my throat, I couldn't speak. What came out was a series of incoherent grunts.

Though, even with all the fright, Jake dressed like a lumberjack with his green plaid shirt rolled up on his forearms and his dark jeans, was the balm this day needed.

"Ainsley? Honey. Tell me what's wrong."

"Truck," I said hoarsely. "Truck?"

"What truck? Were you in an accident?" He started pushing my sleeves up and then checked my head.

"You. Truck." My mouth would not work, no matter how hard I tried. Maybe the cold had frozen my brain. My teeth were chattering.

"Oh. *My* truck is at home. I ran over to wrap your outdoor pipes. A bad storm's coming. Come on, let's get you inside."

"My car," I said. "Intruder."

He chuckled. "I'm sorry I scared you. I just came inside to check the furnace. I wanted to make sure you were set for tonight."

Putting an arm around my shoulders, he hugged me. Then, he sat me on the couch. "I'll let George out, and then I'll go get your car. It sounds like you left it running."

"Getaway." As I mentioned, someone has tried to kill me more than once—it can mess with a person's head.

"Oh, so you can make a fast getaway. Got it. Smart thinking." And there it was, the sweetness that was Jake. I was a petrified, bumbling mess, and he always seemed to understand. "I'll be right back. I have something I need to talk to you about."

He frowned, and that pit in my stomach grew deeper. Jake didn't like to talk, especially, about feelings. If I'd been able to talk, I would have asked him to stay and tell me right away. I wasn't sure how much more my poor nerves could take.

The man came over to check your pipes.

That made me laugh. Perhaps, hysterically. The back door shut, and Jake came back through the living room.

"I turned the kettle on in case you need some of your special calming tea. Give me five minutes to get your car in the barn, and I'll be right back."

"Room. I mean, I don't think there's room."

He smiled. "I made space for it."

The barn also served as overflow for inventory I couldn't keep at the store. I tried to keep everything organized, but we'd been so busy, I'd just been loading stuff in there as it came in.

"You're the best," I said, but he was already out the door.

Pull yourself together, Ainsley. No matter what he says, you'll be mature about it.

Sometimes with me, that's easier said than done. Not that I'm immature, but when it comes to relationship stuff—I'm somewhat clueless.

You don't even know if it's relationship stuff.

I unzipped my boots and managed to stand up to put them in the closet. I made some of the calming tea, more because I was freezing than I needed calming down. Besides, it would give me something to do with my hands.

After mixing up a couple of cups of the special brew, I sat them on the coffee table and waited for Jake. The fire was going—he really did think of everything. I desperately tried not to worry about whatever it was he needed to tell me.

"Okay." He sat down in the chair opposite me. Usually, he was right next to me on the couch. He was like my own personal heater this time of year.

"Is this for me?" He pointed to the mug on the table.

"Yes. What is it you wanted to talk about?"

"I have some not-so-great news." He took a sip of the tea.

"Okay."

"So, I know we were going to do our special Valentine's dinner tonight, before everything got crazy with the wedding and the town charity dance you're sponsoring."

Oh. My. I'd totally forgotten about that. I hadn't picked out his gift yet.

I'm such a great girlfriend.

I decorated a few days ago, so at least there was that. And we were going to Dooley's for dinner, which was off, since the restaurant had been closed when I drove by.

"But with the weather—all emergency service personnel are on call tonight. I have to go into the station."

Oh. He had to work. My shoulders sagged with relief.

"I'm sorry. I feel like I'm saying that a lot tonight. The last thing I want to do is disappoint you."

I reached out and put a hand on his knee, and he covered it with his hand.

"No, it's fine. I get it. I truly do. You forget my brother is the sheriff. You have to be ready for anything."

He dropped out of the chair, and onto his knees. He sat my mug down and then he pulled me into a hug so fast, I wasn't sure what happened at first. He smelled of pine and a hint of smokiness, maybe from making the fire. His was my favorite smell.

"You're the first woman in my life who has understood my job." He seemed to think about those words and pulled back a little. "There haven't been that many, and none I love as much as you. Crud. That still sounds wrong. Anyway, thank you for understanding. I feel so bad about having to cancel tonight."

I shook my head. "You don't have to worry about that stuff with me. We can have dinner any night. Besides, Dooley's closed early like everyone else. I'm hoping folks are smart and just stay home. It will be safer for everyone."

He grabbed my hands in his. "I was going to order pizzas and cinnamon strips for you, but I brought in the giant bag of food. I'm assuming that's from Shannon. I put everything in the fridge, except a couple of ham and cheese croissants. I need snacks for later."

I kissed his cheek.

"Take the whole bag for the gang at the station."

"Are you sure? There's chocolate pie in there," he said.

"Well, leave a me a piece of that, but take the rest. I mean it. She put enough food in there for an army, and you guys have a long night ahead. And thank you for taking care of my house."

"Make sure before you go to bed that you run some very hot water through the pipes. It's going to be below freezing for at least forty-eight hours. It's shut all the big cities north of us down. I'll come by in the morning to see how you're doing."

"You don't need to worry about me," I said. "I'll be fine. I apologize for acting like you were a burglar."

He chuckled. "I'm pretty sure you scared me as much as I scared you. I thought someone was after you. Oh, that reminds me."

His eyebrow went up, and I knew where he was headed.

I put a finger against his lips. "Don't. I will not be getting myself into trouble sitting in my living room."

He kissed my finger. "Fine. But Greg called me earlier. Said that they are fairly certain the woman who died was poisoned. Kane will know more in the morning."

How did someone poison her in a locked room? And was she the intended target? Enquiring minds, mainly mine, wanted to know.

But there was no way I could bug my brother tonight.

Jake kissed my cheek. "Just don't go anywhere, okay? It's ridiculous to even try to tell you to leave it to the police. I can see the wheels turning already. Just promise me you won't leave the house."

I nodded.

He shook his head and laughed. "I'm going to need verbal communication."

I touched his cheek. "I promise to spend the next twenty-four hours right here watching television, only stopping to go to bed."

"Okay. And you don't have to lie to me about the sleuthing. I get that it's just your innate curiosity to know things. But I need you to make sure that you keep yourself safe."

I couldn't blame him for worrying. I didn't exactly have the best track record in that regard.

He kissed me again, and then jumped up.

George whined at the back door. "I'll let him in as I leave, and pour his dinner in his bowl."

"Thanks."

After he left, I turned on the television. I needed something I could watch, and search the internet at the same time. I settled on *Captain Marvel*, which I'd seen a hundred times. I live for that moment when she punches Jude Law's character into a rock.

I'm a nice person, but everyone has a dark side.

I sat down on the couch with my laptop, but ended up watching the movie for several minutes, when there was a loud banging on the door. I jumped again.

"It's me, Ains."

"I don't know why I'm so jumpy."

George was in mid-turn before he settled on the couch. It was a Great Dane thing. If he didn't complete three full turns, he had to start over. He looked from me, to the door, and seemed to decide I was safe, as he snuggled into his blanket.

"If you weren't such a great guard dog, I might be offended."

Jake had been around so much lately, that George probably knew his scent and every sound he made.

Come to think of it, George hadn't growled when he ran for the porch earlier. Not once. He was just anxious to see his friend.

I rolled my eyes, and then opened the door.

"Since I took all of your food, this is for you." He stepped inside.

"Pizza? Yum. But you didn't have to do that."

He smiled. After putting the big box on the counter, he turned to me again. "I still feel bad about tonight."

I put my arms around his neck and kissed him.

"Don't be. If I'm honest, finding that body this morning—well, let's just say the adrenaline has worn off big-time.

I'm going to carb load and sack out."

He hugged me. "Okay. I will make it up to you."

I hugged him back. "It's really okay. Up until this Valentine's Day, I always thought it was overrated. But it's fun when you have someone you love."

"Hearing you say that never gets old. You text me if you need anything. The power should be okay, but I put some firewood on the back deck for you just in case."

"Got it. Now, go, and save the dumb people who choose to get out in this mess."

A few minutes later, I was back in front of the television with two slices of pizza and another cup of tea. I opened my laptop, thinking I'd just do a quick search.

I typed in Jasmine Levy. Her candle-making business website came up. It was all very professional. I loved the history section where she explained that recipes came from her grandmother. But there was no new information.

I went back to my search page. A corporate-looking website came up. Listed as the CEO, Jasmine was a strategic corporate restructure consultant. I had no idea what that meant so I read further. Basically, she and her teams helped companies become more viable and successful.

"Holy, moly. She's a big deal." Her list of clients was impressive. She must have started her career when she was still in college—and she had an MBA.

"Who walks away from all that to make candles?"

She'd mentioned the cancer, maybe that had been the thing that had changed her mind.

There was nothing about her retiring. And her company was still in business. There were other consultants listed.

I guess she really was like Shannon and me. We'd both made big changes to follow our dreams.

She only had one social media account, and there hadn't been anything on it for at least three years. The last was a photo of her standing with a man on a yacht in Belize.

She looked really happy.

Even though I'd asked Shannon to look up the dad, I decided to check everyone out.

I typed in *Levy family*.

And there it was. A picture taken a dozen years ago.

Even though she was much younger, it was easy to recognize Jasmine. She stood on a stage with her dad and sisters. And then I read the caption: *Billionaire family man runs for senator*.

Then it hit me. Oh. My. God. Jasmine's dad was Henry Levy, a billionaire several times over. I'd never made the connection between him and the old mill where my store was.

But it had to be the same family.

He didn't just dabble in oil, he was in tech, and had the Midas touch. I remembered reading about him years ago, and then he seemed to disappear from the public eye two years ago.

He'd only served one term as a senator because he had to leave for personal reasons.

I put in the name Levy, and the year he was a senator.

His wife died of cancer a few months into his term. That must have been what made him leave. With five girls to raise, and a big business, maybe it had been too much.

There was a picture of him standing in front of a church

with the girls. It was easy to pick out Jasmine; she'd been a beautiful child.

But after that, there were no more public photos. There were articles about his many businesses, but the children were never visible in any other photos.

Then about a year ago, there were no more articles or pictures about him. There also weren't any news articles about his death, which would have been big news, at the very least, in Houston.

Maybe the family was holding out to do a press release or something. But if Nia was right, he'd been dead at least three days. It would be difficult to keep it a secret that long.

Not with the kind of money they had, though.

Jasmine was so down-to-earth, it was tough to imagine her the daughter of a billionaire. Of course, I wouldn't have guessed she'd been a high-powered business consultant. For someone so young, she'd accomplished a great deal.

My gut had steered me wrong before, but there was no way she was a killer. In fact, I was worried she might be in real danger.

It was too much of a coincidence that he died, and then his second oldest daughter, within days of each other.

That creepy feeling raised the hairs on the back of my neck.

I wonder who inherits his fortune?

Chapter Seven

FIVE HOURS LATER, I stared up at the ceiling. The wind howled around my old house, and every creek sent my nerves jangling.

Normally, I wouldn't allow George to sleep in my bed. Maybe on the floor at the foot of it, but the wind seemed to be getting to him too, so when he jumped up there—well, it was more of a Great Dane climb; they were gangly, awkward dogs—I let him stay. Besides, it was cold and he kept my feet warm.

"So, George, from what I can see, she walked away from her dad and that fortune. She said it was over politics. That doesn't seem a strong enough reason to leave her family, and she obviously loved them. She was very upset today."

George grunted. That was his 'I'm trying to sleep' answer. "It's too late to call anyone and I need a sounding board."

He grunted again and I laughed.

After all the research I'd done, I was no closer to any answers. Her dad was a ruthless businessman, who had invested early in tech stocks and done very well for himself.

And the family still owned the oil company, which was, according to the last reports, still a multi-billion-dollar enterprise.

My brother hated it when I shared my thoughts, but I was willing to take a risk.

I texted him my biggest worry.

What if someone is killing off family members for the fortune?

I attached an article about the tech and oil companies.

I waited but he never answered.

He was probably busy saving lives.

So, I did the next best thing: I texted my friend Kane, the coroner and medical examiner.

Did anyone look into the father's cause of death?

THE NEXT MORNING it was so dark outside that I considered staying in bed. Greg never answered me back, probably because it was two in the morning when I texted him. When I cracked an eye open, George stared at me expectantly from the bedside. His cold nose pressed into my cheek.

"I'm guessing you need to go do your thing outside?"

George barked.

After throwing on a robe and my fuzzy hedgehog slippers, I let him out the back. When he hit the deck, he slid all the way to the end and fell into the grass. He didn't move.

"Oh. No. George!"

I was about to run to him when he jumped up and shook himself. Then he came back to the door and slid again.

"Stop it." I wagged a finger at him. "You're going to break a hip."

He cocked his head at me and then trotted off to the back field. I had a feeling he'd do it at least two more times before he came in, though the sleet was still coming down, and he was never a big fan of cold weather.

I was about to push the button that brings my coffee machine to life, when my cell rang.

"Hey, Shannon."

"Oh, you're up. I figured I'd just leave a voice mail."

I glanced at the clock and saw it was seven, which was normally her busiest time of day at the coffee shop. "What's up?"

"Well, I don't know if you heard, but only essential businesses are to open today. It's a county mandate. The roads are covered in black ice and I worried you might try to come into town."

"Oh. Good to know. I need to text everyone from the store."

"Mike already did that for you. And he made sure the pipes were okay at Bless Your Art. He said if you want him to open the doors, he will, but he doesn't want you to get in trouble with the county."

"Nah. As much as I hate to lose a day of sales, I don't want to encourage people to shop. Besides, if someone slipped on the sidewalk, I wouldn't be able to forgive myself."

"That's what I figured. And, there's one more thing."

"You sound ominous."

"No. It's just that—Jasmine was in here earlier. She is one of four customers we've had so far. It's been the slowest morning ever, which is probably good. That means people are listening and staying home safe.

"Anyhoo, she and I sat down and started talking."

"Oh, and what did she say?"

"That's she's worried the police think she's the prime suspect and she doesn't know if she should get a lawyer or not."

"Did she tell you who her dad was?"

"She didn't mention him, other than she was worried they'd go ahead with the funeral without her. But Houston is shut down as well. No one has ever seen anything like this storm, and it just keeps coming down. And you know Texans can't drive on ice."

True. There weren't enough snowplows to go around because they were seldom needed that far south.

I pushed the button on the coffee maker.

"But I read about her family last night," Shannon said.

"Me too," I admitted.

"Can you imagine walking away from that much money?"

"Not really. She would have been set for life."

"It makes me respect her even more that she had the strength to do that."

I felt the same way.

George tried to open the back door with his big paw. I'd already brought a towel down to help dry him off.

"I've got to put you on speaker while I dry off George. He's been playing in the sleet."

She chuckled.

"I think maybe she should get a lawyer," I said.

I opened the door to let George in, and then I put two fingers up, which was a signal to sit. While he's a fairly well-behaved dog—provided I don't leave him alone for long periods of time—he didn't know a lot of tricks. And he didn't really care to learn any. Sit was about it.

"Really?"

"Well, it's the whole thing about them not knowing anyone else in town except each other. Why else would anyone try to kill her or her sister?"

"You have a point. Have you heard anything from your brother?"

I sighed. "He's determined to make me stay out of this one. But I like Jasmine a lot and I can't imagine she killed anyone. Besides, she was more than an hour away. Though, I've been wrong before."

After drying his paws, I pointed to George's bowl. He started gulping down food, like it might be his last meal.

"I told her we would help her," Shannon said quickly. "I know, I should have talked to you first. But she just seems so sad and heartbroken. I told her that you were good at finding out things. I may have said something like you've cracked more than a few cases and are kind of a legend around here."

I snorted.

We did share a kinship with her, and my gut told me she was a decent person. The worst thing that would happen might be that I'd prove she killed her sister.

"Are you mad? I feel like you're mad."

I laughed. "No, not at all. I just don't know what I can do from here."

"Well, I told her you'd call her later on today. You're good with people. Maybe you can get some information that she hasn't told us yet."

"We'll see."

"Oh, look who's here. Hi, Jake, I'm talking to Ainsley."

I cringed.

"About wedding stuff?" Jake asked. "It's coming up fast."

There was a long pause. Shannon was a terrible liar.

"Yep," she finally said.

There was another long pause.

Darn. I didn't want Jake to know I was snooping a little.

"Okay. Tell her I'll be out to bring her lunch and to let me know if she needs anything from the store."

"Will do," Shannon said. "Do you want the regular order?"

He must have nodded.

"Ains, I'll have to call you back later. It's for the firehouse, which means twelve cups of coffee, and every one of them different."

We said our goodbyes.

It was still early, and I wanted to do a bit more research before I called Jasmine.

But first coffee. Then a shower, and some breakfast.

"I don't know about you, George, but I'd like to think that I have decent instincts and haven't made another killer my friend. So, I guess, for my own sake, I'm officially sleuthing. Just don't tell Greg."

George lifted his head to stare at me.

"Ruhrroo."

"Not uh-oh. This time I'll be careful."

For some reason, he didn't look like he believed me.

Just then, I got a text from Kane.

Poison mushroom. Hard to find. Suspicious.

Wow. I couldn't believe Kane was just offering info like

that. Jake had been right about her dying from poison, but what kind of mushrooms would do something like that?

My phone buzzed again.

Ains. Scratch that. Meant that for Greg.

Too late now, dude.

Nia Levy?

All I got was a frowny-faced emoji.

So Nia was murdered using mushrooms.

Weird.

"George, we have a murder to solve."

Chapter Eight

Later that afternoon I texted Jasmine to see if she might want to talk, but she didn't answer back. After baking some chocolate chip cookies for Jake and the guys at the firehouse, and then another bunch for my brother and the other officers, I sat down at my computer again.

I found Jasmine's shop on Etsy. The reviews were stellar, as was to be expected. One of the reasons she hadn't been in her room the night her sister died, was because she'd decided to make more of her candles, after she'd been locked out.

One review after another commented on how the candles worked for them. There were so many great love stories that I almost believed her candles had some kind of magical mood inducer.

My phone rang, but it was a video call. I was in my unicorn all-in-one, and had put my hair up in a ponytail wet. It was Jasmine, I meant to hit the button that answered without video, but I hit the wrong one.

She appeared worried at first, and then smiled. "I like your pajamas."

"Thanks." I smirked. She of course looked perfectly coiffed and had a red sweater on. "How are you doing?"

The frown came back. "I wish I could go home," she said. "I've been downstairs watching the news but it doesn't look like the weather will let up anytime soon. It's just so frustrating. I mean, I'm not sure how the rest of my family will react to me, but I want to be there for them."

That was the kind of person she was. Even though they all turned their backs on her, she wanted to comfort them. The tightness in my chest loosened a bit.

"That has to be rough. Is there anything I can do?"

She sighed. "Not until this weather warms up. I'm told the roads between here and Houston are a solid sheet of ice. It's treacherous. And there's a huge pile-up on the highway."

I wasn't surprised.

"Did my brother or the medical examiner share what happened to your sister?"

"What do you mean?"

Crud. They hadn't told her how Nia died. And I'd just stuck my big foot in my mouth.

"I was just curious if you heard anything else."

"No."

And it wasn't really my place to say anything. If I hindered my brother's investigation in any way, he'd kill me.

"I wondered if maybe you could answer a few questions for me."

"Anything to pass the time. I feel like I'm coming out of my skin. Mrs. Carmichael is very accommodating but she likes to hover."

"First question, was there anyone in the family you were close to growing up? Maybe, someone who might email or call you if something was up?"

"No one in the immediate family. My cousin Angie would send me texts or photos occasionally. She never understood why my family shunned me.

"And her dad, Uncle Leon, was quite vocal about how my dad treated me. And my sisters love me, but none of them were ever brave enough to go against my dad. Angie and Uncle Leon were the only ones who kept in touch."

I wrote down the names of her cousin and uncle. And made a note to check on the sisters, as well. I didn't want to sound like I'd been researching her all night, so I asked a question that I didn't want to. "What about your mom?"

"She died when I was about twelve. It's one of the reasons Dad was so tough on all of us to be proper young ladies. She was one of those women, who never had a hair out of place. And I remember she smelled like Chanel No. 5.

"Even when she was just hanging around the house she wore a Chanel suit and heels. When she died, none of us suspected she was even sick. I think that's why my dad had a warped view of what a good woman should be. I don't ever remember her complaining about anything."

I stared down at my unicorn onesie. At home, for me, it's all about comfort. Besides, if I tried to wear anything nice, George would just slobber all over it.

"Can you tell me what your sister said and exactly what happened that night?"

She sighed.

"I was there when you talked to Greg, but I want you to sit down and close your eyes. Take a deep breath. And it's just you and me trying to track what happened after you left the diner. No pressure."

"I'll try." She didn't sound like she believed me.

"I want to help you but I need to know as much as possible. The police follow the evidence, and so do I. But in the short time I've known you, I know you haven't done anything wrong. I just want to make sure you aren't in danger, too."

"You just gave me the shivers." Jasmine coughed. "Wait, do you think someone killed my dad? I heard from Uncle Leon this morning. Dad had been ill for a few months, and he died of a heart attack. Do you know something that I don't? Did they figure out how Nia died?"

Darn my big mouth.

"You did not hear this from me. If my brother finds out I said anything, he will make my life miserable."

"I can keep a secret," she whispered. There was a sense of dread in her voice.

"I accidentally saw that poison was involved but that really is all I know."

"Poison? That's awful. Poor Nia." There was a soft sob.

Way to go, Ainsley.

"I'm so sorry. I didn't meant to upset you."

She shook her head. "No. It's okay. I want to know whatever you find out."

"Okay. I understand you are tired of thinking about this, but I need you to take me step by step through the night she approached you."

She took a deep breath.

"I was walking away from you guys when I heard someone say my name. I jumped and was ready to run, but then Nia stepped out and I hadn't seen in her in so long, it took me a minute. Also, those big trees made it impossible for the light from the streetlamp to get through."

"What did she say? Tell me every word."

"She wanted me to know that Dad had passed away. She said she'd tried to call but my number was out of service. Turned out, she had called one of my old landlines. No one but Uncle Leon and Angie knew I'd moved from L.A. back to Houston a year ago."

"Couldn't she ask your uncle or cousin for the number? I just want to understand why she'd drive all the way from Houston to tell you."

"Well, that's the strange part. She said that it had to be in person. That she wasn't sure the house was safe anymore. I didn't tell the police this, but I think she'd been drinking. I haven't seen her in years, but she was acting strange."

"What do you mean?"

"She'd leave off in the middle of sentences. She slurred a few of her words. Over and over, she said, 'Jasmine, I'm so tired. I just can't do it anymore.' But she never told me what *it* was. When I asked, she'd just say, 'I'm sorry I didn't fight for you,' and then she'd start crying. Right before she went upstairs she said, 'Be careful. And Daddy loved you, you'll see.'"

"Why did your sisters—I mean, if he was so tough, why didn't the others leave the nest?"

"Ainsley, do you know how much my father was worth?"

"He was wealthy."

She chuckled but it wasn't a happy sound. "He had Oprah kind of money. People will do awful things for that kind of life. Even live under his thumb. All the money in the world wasn't enough for me to live like that. But my sisters grew up loving nice things, and it's hard to walk away from the only world you know."

"You did it."

"I did. It was one of the hardest things I ever had to do. It had nothing to do with material wealth, and everything to do with my need to live life my way."

I hadn't known her long, but I could see that. "Tell me a little about what it was like when you were still at home."

"Goodness, I've shoved those memories so far away—let's see. We weren't allowed to go to school with other kids. My father was worried we'd be kidnapped. We had private tutors, which wasn't so bad.

"But he insisted on progress reports at the end of every week. The only time we were allowed to speak at the dinner table was when he grilled us about our studies. He was very old-fashioned. He believed children should only speak when spoken to. If we played music that wasn't classical, we'd be in trouble. If we didn't wear what he considered appropriate attire at all times, we were in trouble.

"If any of us dared to defy him, we'd be locked in our rooms for days, with meals served at the door."

"That's awful," I said.

I thought my parents were terrible when they wouldn't let me go to a Green Day concert when I was in my late teens.

"He could be a mean old coot. To him, telling his daughters that they were worthless only built character. When I told him that I planned to go to college, he came unglued. Part of me still wonders if he didn't want me to go because he was worried about my safety. But I also wonder if he was worried I'd never come back once I discovered the real world."

"But you did walk away."

"Yes. And I honestly don't regret it. There's being sheltered and then there's being a prisoner. I had to break free."

"Have you heard from any of your family members about Nia?"

There was another long sigh. "No. None of them are taking my calls. Goodness knows what Dad told them about me through the years. I'm sure they think I killed her. But I didn't have any reason to. I don't know much about solving crimes but motive is important."

She had a point.

"I had no ill will toward my family. I missed them terribly but I wouldn't want to harm any of them."

"Is there anything else you remember about that night?"

"I got her into the B&B. She was a little loud and I was worried she'd wake the other guests. She took off her coat and then curled up on the couch in the front parlor. She was so…I don't know how to describe it. Distraught maybe?

"Whatever was bugging her, she couldn't quite articulate it. I got her some water and she gulped it down. We just sat there staring at one another. I hadn't seen her in so long.

"She reached out and touched my cheek. 'I'm so proud of you,' she said. 'I mean it about Dad. I just can't believe—' and then the rest was gibberish. It was like she forgot how to form words.

"I gave her my key, and then you know the rest. I drove home. I texted my other sisters, but it was late and no one answered me. After making some candles, I finally passed out."

The news that Nia had seemed drunk stuck with me. What if she'd been dosed already with the poison? Maybe the killer was in Houston.

"Oh. No." Jasmine sounded as if someone had shot her puppy.

"What's wrong?"

"I just got a text from my uncle."

"Oh?"

"My sisters are demanding Nia's body. They want to take her home to be buried with my dad."

"The roads are bad; there's no way they can get here."

"They're coming tomorrow morning in the family helicopter. Ainsley, what am I going to do?"

"Stay calm. I'll be there with you."

"What if they really do blame me for what happened?"

"One thing I've learned about killers over the last year, is that they like to blame other people."

I let that hang there for a minute.

"You think one of them might have killed my sister?"

"I have no idea. I'm just saying that those who have something to hide, usually blame the loudest. This is a difficult situation and you need to be careful."

Now, more than ever, I was worried for Jasmine's safety. "I'll come stand by you for moral support."

"Are you sure, Ainsley? My family—they are not always pleasant when they don't get their way."

"All the more reason for me to be there. I'll see you around eight."

I checked the status of the weather. In true Texas fashion, it was supposed to be a high of seventy the next day.

The roads would be clear, and we could reopen the store. I texted Mike to see if he could help Don, our resident Santa, and one of the kindest souls on earth, open tomorrow.

After letting George out, I sat down at my computer and stared at a picture of the family.

I had two big questions. Was the killer after Jasmine or her sister? And did the same person possibly kill her dad?

Though, if the father's death was from an illness, maybe someone was after his fortune. I wouldn't know until Kane answered my earlier question.

It was time to make a few phone calls.

But as I sat down, George did his menacing growl at the back door. Then there was a loud bang outside. George left the door and ran and stood in front of the couch as if he were protecting me.

"Who would be out in this weather?"

I walked to the back door to peek out. The window was frosted up and I wiped it away. I stood there for a moment waiting.

Nothing happened.

I opened the door slightly, and George pushed through and bounded outside. He ran straight for the back fence and barked loudly.

Probably just kids in the woods. They were out of school because of the weather.

I shivered and it wasn't from the cold.

It was just kids.

At least, that's what I kept telling myself.

Chapter Nine

WHEN I ARRIVED at the B&B the next day, Jasmine was pacing in the front parlor. Her trendy clothes were gone, and she wore a classic-cut black suit, with a black blouse underneath the jacket. Her black pumps and messy bun finished the look. She appeared ready to walk down the runway at a Paris fashion show.

"You look…amazing."

She paused. "Thanks. Luckily, I keep this suit with me when I travel, in case I have to do some consulting work on the side."

Rushing forward, she took my hands in hers. "Thank you so much for being here. I'm warning you, though, I haven't seen them in years, but they will argue to the death to get their way. Unless, my dad was around. Then it was his way, whatever it might be."

"No problem. You're in weird situation, and we haven't known each other long, but I've got your back."

She squeezed my hands. "Just thank you. I have friends in Houston, none of whom would want to be anywhere near my sisters."

I laughed. "They can't be that bad. Maybe they've matured with age?"

She shrugged.

"Do they all still live in your dad's house in Houston?"

She nodded. "As far as I know," she said. "Even though it had seemed he mellowed with age, I can't imagine him allowing them to leave the house unless they married—something I don't think any of us has done. At least, that's what my cousin Angie told me."

The front door opened, and high-pitched voices argued over something. Jasmine coughed nervously. The three women turned our way. Each of them was dressed in a different suit, all variations of black.

The shortest one, waved, and then ran toward us. "Oh, Jasmine. I'm so happy to see you. How are you doing?" Then the woman flung arms around her and started crying. The tallest of the three shook her head, and then rolled her eyes.

"Kiara, calm yourself. We are in a public place." That was the tallest one. And her voice was so formal and stilted, she sounded like she belonged in a Regency drama.

"Ebony, you leave her alone. You're not Daddy. You don't get to tell us how we feel about things." That was the middle sister. She looked like Jasmine's twin, except her hair was a reddish-purple.

"It's been too long, sister," Kiara said.

Jasmine nodded. These did not seem like women who were ready to blame her for anything. Quite the opposite. There was real love in the circle of those arms, and in the tears streaming down their faces.

"Ebony, get over here and give our sister some love. We have a lot of making up to do," Kiara said.

Ebony sighed, but joined the women in a big group hug.

Since they didn't look like they were ready kill her, I thought it best to make my exit.

"Wait," Jasmine said. "Sisters, I'd like you to meet my friend Ainsley McGregor. She owns an adorable shop in town, and works with the police as a sort of…liaison. Ainsley, this is Lila, Ebony and Kiara."

I'd been called a lot of things in my life, but that was a new one. I figured that was Jasmine's way of saying, *please don't leave me.*

"It's nice to meet you." I waved at them, as they were all still entangled around Jasmine. "I came by to check on Jasmine. I'm so sorry for your losses. Your family must be reeling."

They nodded my way. And then glanced from me to Jasmine.

"Ainsley, I'd love it if you'd stay. Maybe you can share some details my sisters don't know yet. Why don't we sit down," she said. We sat on the uncomfortable Victorian sofas and chairs in the front parlor.

"Well, I have a question?" Lila said. "Why does Jasmine look like Halle Berry, and the rest of us are showing our age?"

The room erupted in uproarious laughter. Even I couldn't help but smile.

"Stop it," Jasmine said. "You all look like babies to me. And it's our grandma's cream she used back in the day. Remember, she was like eighty and didn't look a day over fifty."

"How did you get the recipe?" Lila asked.

"In that old chest of Grandma's. I've had it forever. But

when I moved back to Houston last year, I pulled it out of storage to use in my new place. At first, I made some of the creams, and then I used the candle recipes. It's turned into a nice little side business for me."

She hadn't said anything about the creams to me. I wanted a jar, or four, of that stuff.

"Wait. You've been living in Houston?" Kiara asked. "Why didn't you reach out?"

Jasmine shrugged. "I didn't want to get any of you into trouble. Dad had reached out a few times and I was trying to mend fences with him. I thought if I could get in his good graces again, I'd be able to see you without interference or someone else being disowned."

"I wondered," Ebony said. "He'd been talking about you the last few months. We were at dinner one night, and out of the blue, he said, 'Sending Jasmine away is my biggest regret.'"

"He didn't send me away, I left." Jasmine said the words softly.

"I tried to ask him about it," Lila interjected. "But he gave me the dad-eye. So, I left it alone. He's not the only one who is sorry about the past. We all are."

Jasmine smirked. "I was worried maybe you thought I had something to do with Nia's death."

The sisters stared down at their hands.

"I see." Jasmine smiled. "And what changed your mind?"

"We talked to Detective Lucy last night. When she called to ask us follow-up questions, we may have asked about you. She explained that you are not a person of interest and have a strong alibi," Kiara said. "It's just—well, she came to see you and then she was dead."

Ahhh. So, my first call to Lucy paid off. While she didn't like me involved in investigations any more than my brother, she was always grateful when I had some sort of insight. I'd told her about the sisters and Jasmine's worries.

"And you have every right to want to see all of us six feet under," Lila added. "But to be honest, Nia had been acting strangely for a couple of months. Like she'd lash out over the littlest things, when normally she was the calmest out of the four of us. And she cried all the time.

"We thought maybe she was having boyfriend trouble. She never brought anyone around, but who would with the way Dad was. She said she could hear us whispering about her, but for once, we weren't. We were just worried about her."

"Dad picked her to run the company," Kiara said, "and she was the vice president the last few years. She was good at her job. You know she was always his favorite, and that was okay. None of us wanted to work with him, but she seemed happy. Until about two months ago, when she started acting weird. Maybe the pressure was getting to her."

Hearing voices. Overly emotional. Maybe, someone was poisoning her for a long time. That might have been what she'd been worried about and felt she could only trust Jasmine. That would make her desperate attempt to get to Sweet River, and Jasmine, make a little more sense.

There was a slight lull in the conversation. "Excuse me. Do you have any idea how Nia found out that Jasmine was here?"

"No," Lila said. "We thought Jasmine was still in L.A., at

least that's the last we heard from Angie."

"She talked to you about me?" Jasmine was surprised by this news.

"It was the only way we could keep track," Lila said. "She'd told us you were going all over the world for bit. That your consulting had taken off."

Jasmine seemed embarrassed. "I've done okay for myself."

"Hmmm," I said.

"What is it, Ainsley?" Jasmine asked.

"Did Nia mention how she found you?"

She shrugged. "She didn't say. But since she was Dad's right-hand woman for so long, maybe she heard it from him. I told him a few weeks ago that I was back in Houston. I had no idea he was sick. He was talking about me coming for a visit and then I didn't hear from him."

I had to know if her father had been murdered, as well.

It was worth looking into with Kane. While the sisters chatted, and shared what had been going on in their lives, I texted Kane.

He texted back: *Can't talk at the moment but will call you later.*

I'm not always a patient person, which sometimes gets me into big trouble.

I sent him a message about what the sisters had said about Nia's behavior the last few months. None of them appeared to be killers, who used poison, but I never trusted assumptions anymore. In my limited experience, almost anyone could be driven to kill.

I needed to find out who had the most to gain by getting the two main players out of the game.

Chapter Ten

FOUR DAYS LATER, I was at the memorial of a billionaire and his daughter. The celebration, as they called it, was taking place at a large, ornate church in Houston. Almost every seat was full. Shannon and I were in the middle of the balcony.

I'd been to a celebrity funeral before, but it wasn't nearly as elaborate as this.

In addition to being a business wiz, with the Midas touch, Jasmine's dad had been a decorated war hero. We'd seen more than one politician come in, and a few celebrities.

"This guy must have traveled in elite circles," Shannon whispered.

I nodded. "That explains the security outside." I'd never had my purse searched at a memorial. The lights flashed, as if a show was about to begin.

Everyone who had been standing sat down quickly, and the noise that had been reverberating off the walls stopped.

Jasmine had called Shannon and me, and begged us to come. I thought it was a bit strange, but I had a feeling she needed to have moral support. When we'd arrived earlier, she'd been near the door, and had ushered us up to our saved seats.

Then she hugged us, sniffed, and begged us to please

come to the house afterward. She started to say something, but someone must have walked up behind us. She stared over Shannon's shoulder with the strangest look on her face. When I turned to see who it was—no one was there.

A spotlight focused on a single figure on stage. It was hard to tell who it was, and then the person held up a microphone, and the most melodic, beautiful sound came from her voice. It sent chills up my arms. Then she turned, and Shannon and I gasped.

The man next to Shannon whispered to the woman with him. "I didn't know Halle Berry could sing."

"That's not her, it's the daughter no one talks about. Black sheep of the family," the woman next to him said. Jasmine's voice was bold and sweet at the same time. And then, a choir, which included her sisters, came out behind her. By the end of the beautiful song, I had tears in my eyes. Everyone jumped up and started clapping and yelling. Again, not something I'd ever seen at a memorial.

The minister came out and said some soul-stirring words. The kind that make you take notice of your life and the choices you make. Several prominent celebrities gave eulogies. It was all very moving.

"This is the best memorial I've ever been to," Shannon whispered.

"Me too."

There was more music, this time by the choir and a different soloist.

The minister returned to give some brief words about Nia. How she helped so many charities, and gave back to the less fortunate and mentored young girls interested in business.

Even though I didn't know her, my eyes blurred with tears.

"The family would like those who wish to continue the celebration of these two beautiful souls to move on to the reception at their residence. The family would like a few moments of privacy, and will join you soon."

People began to file out.

"What should we do?" Shannon asked.

The family didn't move. They probably wanted to say their last goodbyes. At the same time, I didn't want to leave Jasmine on her own.

"Let's just wait for her outside in the vestibule."

By the time we made it downstairs, everyone was gone.

"Do you think the family is still in there?" Shannon asked.

"I don't know." We waited a few minutes to see if anyone came out.

"I'm going to peek inside," I said. The downstairs doors opened onto a dark hallway. But there was a loud booming voice.

I tiptoed down the hallway to the corner so I could peek around.

A video was on a large screen that came down from the ceiling, and Jasmine's dad was talking. I don't know about anyone else, but it always freaks me out a little when the dead speak. Especially, so close to their death.

"I'll only say this. I have one regret in life. That is turning my daughter, Jasmine, out of the house. She dared to speak her mind and stand up for herself. It's one of those things that feels righteous in the moment. But as an old man, I can say it was the wrong thing to do. Never suppress a dissenting voice. Quite often, those are words you need to hear.

"My dear daughters, I hope you can forgive me for being so tough on you. Jasmine, I know it's far from making amends with you, but I'm leaving you all of my worldly possessions, to disperse as you see fit."

There was a collective gasp, mainly from the family sitting in the front pew. I stretched my neck so I could see a bit better. Jasmine had her head down, and everyone in her family was looking at her.

"I'm proud of you, Jasmine. You built a good life for yourself. I would like Nia and you to work together, to keep our family and business strong. You two will take the company far beyond what I could have ever imagined.

"Lila, Ebony and Kiara, you were faithful to me, and for that, I will make sure you are taken care of. But now, I encourage you to follow your dreams. I had it wrong. That's all I can say. I love all of my girls."

The video flashed off and the screen rose.

Just like that, Jasmine was the head of an empire.

From the way they were looking at her, I had a feeling that her family wasn't too happy about that.

Chapter Eleven

JASMINE MET US in the parking lot with another woman. She had bright red hair, and paler skin than me, which is saying something. I was surprised that Jasmine wasn't in one of the limos with her family. "I can't," she said. Then, she started sobbing.

I pulled her into my arms and let her cry against my shoulder. Shannon dug around in her purse and handed us both some tissues. I have this thing, where if someone I care about is crying, I get a bit sniffly as well.

"Tell us what you need," Shannon said.

Jasmine hiccupped, and then dabbed her nose. "I want to go to my house," she said. "It will be like walking into a nest of vipers at my dad's."

Her sisters had seemed to care about her a great deal, but people were strange about money. It was one of the top three reasons people were murdered.

"Are you sure?" the woman with the red hair said.

"Angie, you know how they are. I think we could all use a bit of time."

Oh, that's who she was.

Angie frowned but then nodded. "I get it. Uncle and I will come check on you tomorrow."

I put Jasmine's address into my navigation. She didn't

seem to want to talk, so we stayed silent on the twenty-minute drive to her apartment. The building was a high-rise, with a valet and a doorman.

"Just pull up here. They'll take care of your car." She handed the valet, who opened the car door and called her by name, what looked like fifty-dollar bill. The valet raced around to my side, and handed me a ticket.

"When you're ready to leave, just call down to the front desk and we'll have the car waiting for you."

"Thanks," I said.

We followed her through the elaborate marble foyer of the building, to an elevator. She waved her key card in front of a light, and we raced up to the penthouse. This was not the sort of place I'd expected she might live in when we met. She had more of a gypsy, maybe lived out of a camper, type of vibe.

My stomach grumbled loud—it was almost noon—and it seemed to break the tension. We all smiled.

When the elevator doors opened, I felt like saying, "We aren't in Kansas, anymore," to Shannon. My friend seemed to be equally mystified by all of this.

There were two walls of windows on both sides, and a living, kitchen and dining room, in one large space. The furniture was expensive but comfortable. There were denim sofas with big boho-styled pillows, and the floors were hickory.

"Come in," she said. "Have a seat in the living room. I'm going to call for some food and then I have a lot to tell you. Are you okay with chef's salads? And the chef here makes a killer crème brûlée."

Shannon smiled. "We'll have whatever you're having."

Shannon and I never turned down food.

"Go ahead and take your shoes off. I'm going to put some jeans and my favorite sweatshirt on. I need—"

"Comfort?"

"Yes. That. I'll be back in a minute."

When she came back, she was dressed in old, torn jeans and a fuzzy Harry Potter sweatshirt.

This was more the Jasmine I knew.

Though, looking around her expensive apartment, I had a feeling I didn't really know her at all. Greg had been right about that.

"Are you feeling any better?" I asked.

She sat down in a big denim chair, and pulled her knees to her chin. Without the makeup, she could have passed for early twenties easily. But she'd told me she was my age—early thirties—when we'd had dinner the other night.

"I'm sorry to drag you guys over here, but I had to get away from my family. They probably think I'm nuts. We were lined up to get in the limos, and I just ran away. They were whispering behind my back, all of them were. It's cowardly, but I just couldn't face them."

"Don't worry. We're here for whatever you need."

"What she said," Shannon added.

Jasmine chuckled.

"Do you want to tell us what happened?" I asked.

Shannon's head snapped around so fast I thought she might go Linda Blair on me.

Jasmine didn't seem to notice. She told us about the video and the inheritance.

"Wow," I said, pretending to be surprised. "That must have been another surreal moment for you. Did you have any idea that might happen?"

"Not a clue. I didn't even expect to be mentioned in the will. Let alone—If someone wasn't trying to kill me, they will be now. There's so much money involved that it's mind-boggling."

"Tell us what you're thinking," Shannon said. She always said I was good at getting people to tell me things, but she was equally gifted. "Ainsley said you'd mentioned that something was going on, but you didn't tell her what."

Before she could answer, the doorbell rang. A young kid, with a room service cart, bustled inside. "Ma'am. I have your order. Chef said to tell you he's sorry for your loss. He knows you like his fried mac and cheese, and his cherry cobbler, so he's included both."

She pulled some twenties out of her jean pocket and handed them to him. "Tell Jenson that I'm going to marry him someday." Then she winked.

The kid blushed, but then nodded. "Yes, ma'am."

"Do you mind eating in here?" She motioned to her comfortable but well-appointed living room where we were already sitting.

"Wherever you're comfortable."

"Let's just do it here. Hold on." She went to a closet by the front door, and rolled out a pile of wood pieces. It wasn't until she pulled them apart, that I realized they were small tables.

"Let us help you," Shannon said.

"No, I've got this. I'm just grateful you two are here. I

have friends, even some in this building, but I can't hash out what I need to with any of them. I'm worried maybe insanity runs in my family. Why would my dad do that? He couldn't have been in his right mind."

"You've been through a lot the last week or so, and what happened today—anyone would need to talk after that."

"You're both too kind. I'm not sure what I'd do if I hadn't met you last week."

"We're happy to be here," Shannon said.

I nodded.

"I have wine and champagne, but I mix a mean Arnold Palmer, if you're interested."

I loved tea and lemonade together. "Sounds great."

After she set us up with food and drinks on the small tables, she sat down again in the big chair.

"You should have seen their faces. But let's just say, if looks could kill, I'd be dead about twenty times over. After that video, the whole family stared at me like they wanted to imagine me dead."

"Money does that to people."

"Part of me doesn't blame them. I haven't been around for years, and then suddenly, I'm my dad's biggest regret, and not for any reason I might have imagined? None of this makes sense."

"You mentioned your dad had reached out. What did he say during your last conversation?" I asked. Then I dug into the chef's salad. It was a culinary treasure, and I'm fairly certain I'd never said that about a salad. The turkey and ham had been smoked, and the cheese, it was perfection.

"That he was proud I'd struck out on my own and become successful. I mean, that's how he measured his life, by success. But I'm not like him. I was passionate about helping people, and I look at the world differently than most do in business. It's how I was able to—"

"Afford a place like this?" Shannon blurted out. Her face, when she'd realized what she just said was priceless. "I did not mean to say that out loud."

"Happens to me all the time," I said.

Jasmine couldn't stop laughing. "This is why I wanted you guys here today. The other night at Dooley's, it was like being back in L.A. and hanging with my friends. They didn't know about my family, or care who I was. And I feel like you two are the same way."

"We are," I said. "We are here for whatever you need."

"Except two weeks from tomorrow," Shannon said.

I had to stop and think. "Oh, yes. We will definitely be busy that day. Someone—" I pointed at Shannon "—is getting married."

"Did I tell you I met Mike?" Jasmine asked. "You are so lucky, Shannon. He was kind and helpful. I was trying to restock, and he could see I had a problem. I told him I needed some type of blocks or something to vary the heights. He came back with some large wooden blocks from the toy booth. They worked perfectly."

Shannon sighed happily. "That's my man. The great thing about him is he would have helped you even if you didn't look like Halle Barry."

We snorted with laughter again. At this rate, I was going to die by choking on lettuce, which was an extremely sad way to go.

"And, Shannon, you're right about the apartment. It's not really me. I mean, I decorated it like me, but I don't belong in a high-rise with a doorman. This was a big, look-at-me-Dad-I'm-successful choice. It's very difficult to get into this building.

"But I still had friends from my old life here. And it's weird, a year ago that was so important to me—for my dad to know I was successful. But I swear, I'd give it all up to talk to my dad and sister again."

"That's completely understandable," Shannon said. "But now, I mean, you have an empire to run. So, you're probably stuck here."

Jasmine frowned, and then shook her head. "I don't think I want to stay here. I most certainly don't want to run my dad's corporation. I'm good at finding the best people for the job, and then I'll check in on them. I still run my company that way; I'm just not taking on new clients myself."

"You should move to Sweet River," I blurted out. "Once you get things settled. You have family ties there and, I'm being totally selfish, but it would be great to have you nearby."

She smiled and this one went to her eyes. "I love that you have your own artist colony there. And there's not a single cookie-cutter house in town. I wonder if my gran's old place is still in the family trust."

"Do you know where the house was?" I'd been so busy researching her family online, I'd forgotten about her ties to the place.

"I honestly can't remember. I just know it looked like a

giant gingerbread house. It had so much detail on the front."

"That sounds like Sweet River," I said. "We have a lot of German, Gothic and Victorian architecture."

"I've been looking for a place that feels like home," she said.

"I told you the other night that I moved there from Chicago," I said. "I'd been a city girl all my life. I wasn't so sure about small-town living, but the friends I've made—I never want to leave."

"Me neither," Shannon said. "You should totally move to Sweet River. We'd all have so much fun together."

"We would," Jasmine said.

"What are you going to do about all the business stuff?" Shannon asked.

"I can't wrap my head around it. I have to talk to the lawyers in the morning. I have to meet them at my dad's office tomorrow. So, I'm not thinking about that until tomorrow. Once we get through the paperwork... I don't suppose I could talk you two into staying over?"

Shannon and I glanced at each other. We'd brought overnight bags, thinking we might stay at a hotel and do a little shopping the next day.

"It's too much to ask. You both have extremely busy lives to get back to. You don't need to be wasting your time holding my hand."

"We can stay," Shannon said. "We were planning on spending the night in a hotel and leaving tomorrow. It's not a problem."

"Bless you both. I have this horrible movie in my head where the lawyers are talking to me and all I hear is whaaa whaa whaa. I just want someone else to be there to make sure I don't miss anything. Dad wanted Nia and me to run the corporation together. It's—I can't believe she's gone." Jasmine sniffed.

"We will do our best to pay attention and we are here for whatever you need. I can't even imagine what you must be feeling."

"I really am going to owe you two when all this is over."

I shook my head. "You two would be there for me."

They agreed.

"Oh, you said something strange was going on at your family's house?" I couldn't remember exactly how she phrased it. "That you worried insanity might run in the family?"

"I don't know what to think. My sisters asked me to stay at the house with them last night, so we could all go to the memorial together. That was weird and overwhelming at the same time. I mean, it looked almost exactly the same. At first, I thought maybe it was the stress of being there. All of those memories came crashing in on me."

"What do mean by *it*?"

She chewed on her lip. "I'm almost afraid to say it out loud because I know how it sounds."

"No judgments from us," I said. "We've been involved in enough of these cases that nothing surprises us anymore."

She put her fork down. "Do you remember when I said that Nia kept telling me she was tired?"

We nodded in unison.

"Right before she went upstairs, she said she didn't want to hear the voices anymore. But when I asked her what voices, she never answered."

She chewed on her lip again.

"Tell us," I said quietly.

"Dad turned my room into a conference room because it was close to his study. At least, that's what Lila told me. So, I stayed in Nia's room."

"And?" Shannon whispered.

"I heard voices. And then I swear I saw Nia at the end of the hall early this morning. I didn't sleep well, and needed coffee. I said her name, and she turned and ran down the stairs. I ran and looked over the bannister but no one was there."

We were quiet for a bit.

"Maybe, we turn a certain age and the mental illness kicks in?" Jasmine asked. Her face was tense and she wrung her hands.

She seemed perfectly sane at the moment. "Did anything else happen while you were there?"

"I had a headache the whole time. I get stress headaches easily. It's one of the reasons I made candles. The aroma therapy helps. But my mind was foggy, until we got to the church."

"Who planned all of that? The memorial, I mean."

She blinked. "Everything, except the song at the beginning, was a part of my dad's instructions for his memorial. But the singing was the only thing Nia wanted. When we were kids, we used to harmonize on hymns. I was scared to death. I've never sung in public—well, except for that one time at karaoke, but I'd had a lot of mojitos. But I will do anything for my sisters."

"She wanted you to sing, which meant she must have known about you and your dad making amends."

"I guess. But she probably thought she wouldn't be dying for another fifty years or so. Is this your way of avoiding telling me I'm crazy?" She stared down at her food.

"Oh. Goodness. No. But I'm fairly certain we should get you a blood test. I think someone gas-lighted poor Nia. I'm texting Greg that the police need to do a more thorough search of your dad's house.

"And I don't know the full coroner's report. I need to talk to Kane to see if there is a possibility that she'd been ingesting poison over a length of time. If so, it should show up in her organs. Until the police check it out, you need to stay away from your family and that house."

"You're saying someone in the family did this to my sister?"

It had to be said. "Yes. There's also a possibility they killed your father. It's just too suspicious that their deaths were so close together."

She gasped. "I can't believe it."

"And I think you could be next."

Chapter Twelve

WE ENDED UP staying overnight in Jasmine's opulent guest bedroom. It was like staying at a resort. "I know she says she wants to move, but I wouldn't." I had just come out of the steam shower and still had a towel wrapped around my hair. I wore one of the robes Jasmine had hanging on the bathroom door. "Those soaps in her shower are from Paris. And that shower—my sinuses have never felt so good."

We laughed.

"What about that dinner last night? The prime rib, and those garlic mashed potatoes. We need to walk a lot today or I won't fit in my wedding dress. Can you imagine having that kind of service at your fingertips?"

"I couldn't live like that. They'd have to roll me out of the door with a wheelbarrow. I'm not sure I'd be able to stop calling down for amazing food."

"I wonder what will happen today. She doesn't want anything to do with that company. You can tell, right?"

"Yep. But I'm not sure she's going to have a choice."

I stopped and turned around. "What if the murderer or murderers were also gas-lighting the dad? Maybe that's why he reached out to her, and why he left her the company. Jasmine was the only one in the family he could trust. Maybe he was aware something hinky was going on."

Shannon pursed her lips. "Hmmm. You may have something there."

A knock on the bedroom door made me jump.

"Breakfast is here," Jasmine said.

I opened the door. She was dressed in jeans and boots, and a green sweater that was just gorgeous. "Morning," I said.

"When you finish up, come have breakfast with me. We have some time before we meet the lawyers."

I twisted my wet hair and pulled it up into a bun. It was the easiest way to dry it, so it didn't frizz.

Breakfast was just as impressive as lunch and dinner. We'd just finished when the valet buzzed that Jasmine's car had arrived.

"We'll be right down," she said.

"I could have driven us over," I said.

"The company sent the car. I'd planned to drive myself but I received a text saying they would pick me up. It's one of the perks of being a CEO, which I'm not yet, but whatever. We should go."

A SHORT TIME later, the car pulled up in front of gleaming skyscraper that sparkled with sunlight. It was so bright I had to pull my sunglasses out of my purse.

"Hello, Ms. Levy, please go on up." He cleared his throat. "Your, um, office is on the top floor." He pulled a key card out of his pocket. "You can use this, and your private elevator is the last one on the right."

"Thank you, Jeffrey," she said.

He seemed taken aback that she knew his name, but it was on his shirt.

The lobby was all marble floors and walls with a large wall fountain behind the reception desk.

As we made our way to the elevators, I was glad we were with her. This place was daunting.

She stood with her finger hovering over the button to open the elevator.

"Are you okay?" I whispered.

She took a deep breath. "Once I go up there, everything is going to change."

"Yes." I put a hand on her shoulder. "But just like before, you're in control. You get to decide how you handle this."

"What she said," Shannon offered. "Let's do this."

She pushed the button and the doors opened immediately. We zoomed up so fast, I felt a bit nauseous.

When the doors opened, a woman dressed in a black suit and librarian glasses was there to meet us.

"Ms. Levy, we're happy to see you. I'm Lavinia. I was Nia's assistant. I understand that you will most likely want to bring in your own staff, but I'd like to help facilitate the transition."

"Lavinia, you called Nia by her name, right?"

"Yes, ma'am."

"Please do the same with me." She held out her hand to shake the assistant's. "I'm Jasmine and these are my associates Ainsley and Shannon."

We all shook hands.

"It's nice to meet you." Lavinia smiled but it was obvious from her clammy hand that she was nervous. "Let me show you your fath…I mean, sorry, your office and conference area. I took the liberty of setting up a continental breakfast. Your sister liked people to be full, so they were less cranky."

She sniffed, and turned her head away. "I'm really going to miss her." Her voice was coarse with emotion. "Apologies again. I still haven't wrapped my head around the fact she's gone."

"We understand," Jasmine said sweetly. "I'm sure many of you are wondering about the future of the company. I don't want to worry you. Help me spread the word that there will not be any immediate changes. Their jobs are safe."

"Thank you," she said. "That will be welcome news to many."

We followed her. Nia's nameplate was on the office next to what had been their father's. If I could find out who she talked to that last day, it might help with the investigation into Nia's death.

I had to get into that office.

For the next hour, we sat around a conference table, while the lawyers took Jasmine through the paperwork and the will. It was no wonder she was good at her consulting job—she seemed to understand everything, in regard to the business, better than the lawyers.

They were impressed by her, as were Shannon and I. We were listening but also texting one another as to how out of our depth we were.

Running to the ladies', I texted Shannon about what I was planning to do.

Her eyebrow went up and she smiled.

Be careful and SOS if you need help.

Outside the conference room, the assistant's desk was empty. I tried the door of Nia's office but it was locked.

Things are never that easy. I don't know why I was disappointed.

I went back to the assistant's desk and I'm not sure what I thought I might find. There was a set of keys on the desk but there were several others on there. I picked them up and headed back to the door. Greg told me once that many keys and locks have the same logo, so I looked for that and found it much more quickly than I expected.

After taking a quick look around, I slipped inside.

Most people put their calendars and schedules online these days, but lucky for me Nia had a datebook. It was still opened to the day she died.

There were several notes, and a few names. I typed them into my phone. The second part of the day was blank except lunch with Uncle Leon. And then, the website for Jasmine's candle business. So, she had been looking for her.

But something had happened between her lunch and when she finally found Jasmine. Uncle Leon. Could he have poisoned her at their lunch? He'd seemed protective of Jasmine, and she said he fought for her. So, why would he want to kill her?

I flipped a few pages earlier in the week. She had a list of names, and then question marks. They were her sisters' names. Did she suspect they killed her father?

And did they kill Nia?

I'd met the sisters. They seemed more logical suspects.

My phone buzzed.

Get out. Lavinia's coming back.

Shannon had decided to be the lookout. Thank goodness, I'd forgotten I wasn't supposed to be in here. I snapped a quick picture of the list, and then slipped out.

Shannon and the assistant were talking as they walked down the hall. I'd almost forgotten the keys, and quickly dropped them on the desk.

WHEN I RETURNED to the conference room, I don't think any of them even realized Shannon and I had been gone. By the end of the meeting, Jasmine smiled. "Okay. I kind of see why Dad wanted me to work with Nia. The corporation is going through some changes but this is in my wheelhouse."

The lawyers nodded. "With your business acumen, you'll be able to work with his many holdings, and figure out how to move forward with each one."

"Right. It's the same sort of thing I've been doing for clients. Only, now, I'm doing it for my family."

"And this last set of papers talks about your trust."

She'd been smiling, but her face fell. Her eyes were watery.

"What's wrong?"

She sniffed. "This trust was set up when I was seventeen."

Shannon and I glanced at each other. We had no idea

why that mattered.

"Is that a problem?" I asked.

"On my seventeenth birthday, I'd already graduated high school, and I had scholarships for college that spring semester. Dad couldn't tell me what to do anymore. I walked out of the house with the clothes on my back, a box of books, a stuffed bear my mom gave me, and my grandmother's trunk. And I never looked back."

One of the lawyers pointed to something on the document.

"Two weeks later—" she held up the paper "—Dad set up a thirty-million-dollar trust for me. So that if anything ever happened to him—Oh, Daddy."

She started sobbing. The lawyers looked uncomfortable, so Shannon jumped up. We hugged her.

"He loved me. This must have been what Nia was talking about."

The older lawyer cleared his throat. "I put together that trust," he said. "Your father said that out of all his daughters, you would be the one to make the family proud. When he made these changes, putting you at the head of the company, do you see the dates?"

She grabbed some tissues that had magically appeared in Shannon's hand, and then took the paper from him. "I didn't notice before. This was the day I got my MBA."

The lawyer smiled. "He'd always meant for his company to be yours. You had the best heart. That's what he said when we put all of this together."

"I can't believe this. I—it's too surreal. But what about my sisters?"

That right there. That was why I didn't think Jasmine had anything to do with her sister's death. She was always looking out for other people.

"He left trusts for all of your sisters. And he's asked that they be allowed to live in the house as long as they want. While they don't have the money and power that you do now, they will be taken care of. But you are the executor of their trusts. They will have to come to you if they need more than their yearly allowance."

That probably wouldn't be fun for her. I hadn't spent much time with the sisters but they seemed kind of high-maintenance.

"Well, here's my card," the older gentleman said. The younger one handed over his as well. "We are here to help make the transfer as easy as possible. It's a living will, so there is no probate. Everything was put into a trust for you.

"If I were you, I'd speak to Leon soon. Your father had entrusted him with the majority of the business the last year, and as you can see, all of the companies have been doing well."

What if Leon thought he was taking over the company? That might upset him. And he did have opportunity to slip poison to Nia.

"I will," she said.

I couldn't help it. I had to ask the lawyers what had been on my mind since about halfway through the meeting.

"If something had happened to Jasmine, who would have taken over?"

"I'm sorry, I can't answer that," the older man said. "Client privilege and all that."

Jasmine stood and put her hands on her hips. "I'm curious about that as well, and I am the client."

The two men looked uncomfortable. The youngest one cleared his throat. "It was Nia. And after that, it was to be divided equally between your sisters and your uncle Leon."

And there we had motive.

Nia was dead.

So, if something happened to Jasmine…

"Well. That's a bit scary," she said.

"You need to be very careful, and stay away from your family," I said.

Chapter Thirteen

TO GET JASMINE'S mind off of everything, Shannon and I took her to some funky stores to do a bit of shopping. I was on the hunt for the perfect gift for Jake. I had a sweater, but I wanted to do something a bit more personal.

When we returned, Angie and an older man waited for us in the lobby.

"Uncle Leon." Jasmine threw her arm around him.

"Hello, little dove."

She sighed happily.

If he was the killer, she was about to be very disappointed.

"A little retail therapy is good for the soul," Angie said as we rode up the super-fast elevator again. She looked nothing like her father, and I was curious about that.

"I've never been much of a shopper," Jasmine said. "But I have to admit, it did help clear my head. I think I just needed to get out for some fresh air."

"You've had a lot to deal with the last few days," Leon said. "But I have a feeling your days of being able to go out like that are numbered."

He sounded so ominous. Shannon and I glanced at one another.

Was that a threat?

"Why is that?" Jasmine asked.

"Unfortunately, the press got wind that you're taking over."

"You're the newest billionaire, and everyone is going to want a piece of you," Angie said.

"Angie!" her father admonished. "Jasmine, you need to be careful. Do not travel without security. Don't go out alone—that sort of thing."

Jasmine sighed. "You sound like my father when we were kids."

"You had no idea what was going on," he said. "There were constant threats of kidnapping. We even had a couple of scares in the early days. It's why your father was so protective."

"I…didn't know." She looked like she wanted to say more.

She'd been through more than one shock today. After years of thinking her father hated her, she discovered that wasn't the case at all.

I couldn't imagine how she might be feeling.

The doors opened and we piled inside her penthouse.

"We should head home," Shannon said. "That way you can visit with your family in private."

"Oh, I forgot to introduce you. Uncle and Angie, these are two of my dear friends Ainsley and Shannon. They live in the town where Grandma Johnson had her house."

"Sweet River," said Leon. "Lovely place. Always forward in its thinking. I lived there with my brother until we went away to school. That's also where he met his beloved wife."

"It's still that way," Jasmine said. "It's a very artsy place."

"Well, it's nice to meet you both," Leon said. "Thank you for looking out for our Jasmine."

"It's been our pleasure," Shannon said. "We'll just grab our stuff, and get out of your hair."

Shannon didn't know about my suspicions. I didn't want to leave Jasmine alone with her uncle. He seemed like a nice enough guy but someone was knocking off her family members.

"Stay," Jasmine said. "Please? Just until tomorrow?"

I glanced at Shannon. I couldn't believe she wasn't freaking out more about her wedding.

"Um. Let us drop these off in the room. We'll be right back," I said.

We dumped our shopping bags in the guest room.

"Give me a few minutes to see if I can get someone to cover for me tomorrow," Shannon said.

"I need to do the same, but are you sure?"

She smiled. "She's our friend and she's been through more than either of us can imagine. It's like one of those Lifetime movies and you wonder when the poor woman is ever going to get a break. If someone is trying to knock off her family members, well, we need to keep her safe."

"But you had every hour of every day accounted for in your wedding countdown notebook. I don't want to stress out another friend, by helping someone else."

She put her hands on my arms. "Ains. This is terrible to say, because of the circumstances, but getting out of town for a few days hasn't been the worst thing. My world can get very small at times. Helping someone else is just what I needed. Besides, you've met me. I'm ahead of schedule. All that's left is making sure the venue is coming along okay. I literally have everything taken care of, so that I can show up and enjoy the day."

I laughed. "I should have known you were ahead."

"Right? And I know you don't want to leave her alone. This is…crazy pants. Let's get out there and talk to the cousin and uncle. We need to find out things, like, is Angie adopted?"

"Shannon!"

"I don't mean it like that. But she doesn't look like anyone else in the family. She's a bit rough around the edges. I know how that sounds. She just doesn't seem to fit in with the rest of the family."

Shannon wasn't wrong.

"We need to remember that those two people are the only ones who kept in touch with Jasmine the last few years."

She nodded. "But that doesn't mean you can't do a bit of your Ainsley McGregor sleuthing."

My friend knew me a little too well.

"There is one thing I need to tell you." I explained about the datebook and what I'd found.

"I was wondering what you'd found. So Nia had some idea of what was going on."

I nodded.

"Well, then, we have to stay."

As we stepped out into the hall, I caught a glimpse of Angie going into the bathroom at the end of the hall.

Had she been listening to our conversation?

Shannon glanced back at me. "I'm a terrible person."

"The door was shut," I whispered. "I'm sure she didn't

hear anything."

We joined Jasmine and her uncle. They were talking about the business.

"Hey, you two. Are you staying?"

I nodded.

The relief on her face was worth any inconvenience.

"I was about to grab a couple of bottles of wine. Do you want some?" she asked.

"Sure, but why don't we get it for you," Shannon said. "Do you want the bottles that are on your island?"

"Yes, and thank you."

We grabbed some wineglasses and were in the kitchen when Angie walked through.

"Have y'all been friends with Jasmine for a long time?" she asked. She stared down at her nails, which were painted red, and had rhinestones all over then. They were so long and pointy, I wondered how she texted people.

"It seems like forever," Shannon said.

Clever girl. I liked that she knew not to give too much away.

"Well, I just wanted to say thanks. Like my dad said, we really appreciate you guys looking out for her. She's always been one of my favorite people. The rest of the family always treated me like an outsider because I was adopted. But she never did. I love her like a sister."

Well, that answered *that* question.

"She is special."

I felt terrible. Angie was a nice person and probably did feel like an outsider.

"Leon seems like a nice guy," I said. He seemed to genuinely care about Jasmine, but I needed to know more.

Angie's smile brightened. "Best dad ever," she said. "He and my real dad were best friends. They were in the Gulf War together. My dad asked him to look out for the family if anything ever happened to him.

"He never made it home. And my mom didn't want to take care of me by herself, so Leon stepped in and adopted me. The red-headed white baby. He was single, can you imagine? I owe him everything."

It was strange that she'd shared her life story with us and I worried she'd heard us talking about her.

"That's a beautiful story," I said. And bad guys didn't normally adopt a friend's orphaned child.

"It makes me kind of sniffly," Shannon added.

We took the wine out to the living area, and had a perfectly lovely afternoon with Angie and her dad. They were kind and funny people. They had such a great father-daughter relationship. Every once in a while, Jasmine would glance at them with a wistful look in her eyes.

Neither of them came across as killers but I couldn't be sure.

The problem was tomorrow we had to head back to Sweet River, and it would be impossible to investigate them further.

AFTER THEY LEFT, I was ready to head to bed. But I had my nosy hat on and I had questions.

"They seem to care about you a great deal," I said.

"My uncle made sure I had everything I needed when I went to college. He took me shopping and bought me clothes because he knew I couldn't afford them. I had no money back then. My dad made sure of that."

"Didn't he get in trouble with your dad?"

She smiled. "He never said a word about it and I certainly didn't. Through the years, I'd touch base with him and Angie. She lived with me for a little while when I was out in Los Angeles."

"Oh?" Shannon said.

"Yes. She thought she might try acting but it didn't work out. She ended up in rehab—Oh, I shouldn't have said that."

"Secret circle," I said. "You never have to worry about that sort of thing with Shannon and me."

She smiled. "Well, she seems to have pulled herself together the last few years. I'm proud of her."

"I need to ask you something and it isn't easy," I said.

She stood up. "I have a feeling you want to know if I have some idea who killed my sister? And the answer is: I have no idea. I haven't spent a lot of time with my family but it's difficult for me to believe one of them could have done this."

"What about your uncle?" Shannon asked. "I mean, he seems really nice but he was on the list of people who get the company, right?"

I thought Jasmine might get upset but she just walked over to the window and stared out.

"I don't know any of them well enough, really. My uncle and I mainly stayed in touch by phone the last few years. It hurts to think anyone in the family would do this."

"I'm scared for you. Please be careful."

Shannon was right. More than ever, Jasmine was in danger.

Chapter Fourteen

AFTER STOPPING ON the way home at Junk Gypsy, where I may have overindulged with some super cute tops and bedding for my guest room, we had lunch at Teague's Tavern in Round Top.

"Is it me, or does it feel like we've been gone for two months?" I said as I pulled out on the highway.

"That was a lot of drama for two days. At least her uncle seems nice."

"He did. But why does that whole family look like celebrities?"

"You know what's freaking me out right now?"

"What?"

"That two weeks from today, I'll be walking down the aisle."

"But you're freaking out in a good way, right? No cold feet?"

"Oh, gosh, no. Not about marrying Mike."

"So is it all the details?"

"Nah. That's one of the reasons we kept everything very simple. We have a great place, wonderful caterers, a cake from that new bakery. Sheila is a genius. We can decorate the barn early, so there's no rushing."

I chuckled. "Okay, so why are you freaking out?"

"Because I'm not nervous, like at all. I'm a little worried about my family. Mom is super religious, and doesn't like the idea that her oldest daughter is getting married in a barn—but other than that, I'm calm. I feel like I should be a basket case. But after the past two days with poor Jasmine, any troubles I might have are mild in comparison. I mean, someone may be trying to kill her for a whole lot of money. It's scary."

"Exactly. Maybe we shouldn't have left her there," I said. "But short of dragging her to the car, I didn't know what to do."

"And then, all those reporters and paparazzi in front of her building. Her life has changed big-time," Shannon said.

News of Jasmine taking over had been leaked to the press. There were reporters staked out on the street across from her apartment building.

"It's a lot for one person to take on," I said. "We need to find out who the killer is so she'll be safe."

"I agree. I liked her uncle and cousin, but I'm guessing you think anyone in her family could be guilty."

"You're right. Though I'm thinking it is probably someone in the house. They had to have opportunity. Maybe it's one of the sisters, or maybe they're all involved. It's tough because they're in Houston, and I'm here. I wish I could have gone to their house."

"Well, maybe we just have to be clever," Shannon said.

"I'm thinking about snooping in my brother's files. There have to be interviews with the family. Maybe, I'll see something there."

As we pulled into town, I sighed. A happy one. I love

where I live. It's my happy place.

"I've relied heavily on my crafters the last several days. I need to get back to work. And poor George. I don't think I've been away from him this long ever. His separation anxiety has to be going through the roof."

Though, when Jake called me the night before, George was sacked out on the couch with his head in Jake's lap.

"We have the Valentine's dance next week," Shannon said. "Maybe we should have invited Jasmine. It might be an excuse to get her here."

I laughed.

"What?"

"Great minds and all that. I invited her. She said she'd think about it."

"Cool."

"Usually, by now, you'd have some idea who the killer is," Shannon said out of nowhere.

"And I'd probably be wrong. This is one of those times when there are too many suspects. Until I get some information from my brother and Kane—I mean, I have an idea. That maybe, just maybe, there are two different killers. What if Nia killed her father? But then, why would someone be trying to drive her crazy? I've never been more confused."

"Well, it's definitely not the uncle," she said.

"I have to admit, he seemed to be truly worried about her. And he listened when she shared her story about being in the house. He gave her the same advice we did: to stay away from there."

"I didn't get to meet the sisters, but you did. Could it be one of them?"

I sighed. "I'd like to say, no. I mean, they argue but many sisters do. I mean, look at how Greg and I treat each other. We're constantly teasing and bickering."

"Usually because you get involved in his cases and he wants to keep you safe."

"There is that. We're talking about billions here. It could be someone who works for them. It could be a competitor. But those voices—they'd been trying to scare her. Which reminds me, I wonder if my brother ever contacted the Houston police. They need to search every nook and cranny of that house."

It was all tied to those voices. The person who was gaslighting family members had to be the killer. But who?

"Or it's a setup," I said.

"You've lost me," Shannon said.

"Whoever was doing this, wanted to make it look like Jasmine killed Nia. Maybe, they didn't know that Jasmine had gone back to Houston that night?" I shrugged my shoulders. "This is giving me a headache."

Shannon laughed. "Me, too. I feel like we're missing something that's obvious."

"Might be time to use the whiteboard, but we can't tell anyone. Okay? I don't want my brother to find out—I'm just not in the mood to listen to his lectures. But we have to find the killer fast. Otherwise, poor Jasmine will never be safe."

"Um. Ainsley?"

"Yeah?"

"What if that person saw us at the diner that night? Maybe they'd been following Nia, and then they saw Jasmine with us."

"I'm not following."

"I know it sounds crazy, but maybe they were trying to frame her."

The adorable bride-to-be might have a point.

"Hmmm. My brother and his team wouldn't have been looking for another car. I'll look into that. I may just start calling you Watson."

She laughed. "I'd totally be okay with that."

I hoped Jasmine agreed to come for the Valentine's Day dance. It was the only way I knew we could keep her safe.

Chapter Fifteen

ONE THING SWEET River loves more than anything is a festival. Every holiday, including Valentine's Day had one. This was the first time since Christmas for people to get out and about. Though much smaller than our Christmas one, many of our favorite vendors were back. Luckily, this time, someone else was chairing it, so I didn't have that responsibility weighing me down, which is good since I had been called into the principal's office.

"Do you guys have it handled?" I asked Maria and Carrie, who manned our booth.

"No worries, boss," Carrie said. "Don and Mrs. Whedon are in the store, and we're good for the next few hours."

Maria and I laughed.

"Carrie, some day you are going to take over the world," I joked.

"Shhh," she said. Then she steepled her fingers together and waggled her eyebrows. "Don't reveal my evil plan." She laughed evilly, which was pretty funny.

"I'll be at the police station talking to my brother. Feel free to text me and say you need me to come help right away. I could use an out."

"I'll give it twenty minutes, and then I'll text you," Carrie said.

"You really are my favorite."

"Hey." Maria pretended to be upset.

"It's okay, Mom, someone has to be the favorite."

Those words... Something clicked in my brain.

"Thanks again, I'll see you soon. Come on, George." We took off toward the station at a fast pace. George was still punishing me for leaving him.

"Slow down, dude." I can't run without having some sort of cardiac event. Well, I assumed since exercise wasn't my friend, that might happen. My doctor said something completely opposite, but I didn't believe her.

As we walked away, I had that strange feeling that someone was watching me. I turned around and put my hand over my eyes. But nobody looked my way.

"Weird," I said. While I didn't always get it right with suspects in a case, my spidey senses were usually on target.

I looked back over the crowds again, but didn't see anything out of the ordinary.

Maybe it was the case giving me the willies.

No one was at the front desk of the police station and the lobby was empty. I'd never seen it like this. It was kind of spooky.

"Greg?"

George sniffed the air, but he wasn't growling. At least there was that.

"Greg?" I said louder. My voice trembled and my hands shook.

Still, no answer. I didn't know if I should wait in the lobby, or head back to his office. George made the decision for me, as he yanked me toward my brother's office. He wasn't there, but the door was open. I sat down in one of the chairs across from his desk. George settled in a dog bed my brother kept for him in the corner.

When Greg didn't show up after a few minutes, I closed the door. The files from Nia's case were on his desk.

I was about to text him, when my phone dinged.

Greg texted me: *Emergency call. Be about 45 mins.*

I could walk back to the festival, but that was a whole two blocks away. Or I could sit and take a look at the files. They couldn't be that important if they were out on his desk and the door was open.

Or he left in a hurry.

I decided my conscience could take a nap. It was my duty to make sure my friend Jasmine was safe. That meant we needed to find out as much as possible.

The first file held statements from each of the family members. I didn't know if it was just the notes the officers had taken, but the sisters hadn't been very helpful. As in, they kept saying to almost every question: I don't know.

An officer had made a note that their admission about Nia's behavior seemed rehearsed. As if, they'd all decided to tell the exact same story.

Red flags waved in my brain. They, more than anyone else, had motive and opportunity.

Each sister's credit report held interesting information. Ebony had just bought a new Bentley several weeks ago. Did she know she'd be getting her inheritance?

Lila had put money down on a condo in the Cayman Islands. After living with her family for so many years, I didn't blame her for wanting her own place. But it was the timing. She too, had made the purchase a few weeks ago—before her father died.

Kiara had bought clothes, but it wasn't anything she hadn't done in the months before.

Maybe Lila and Ebony were in on it. Since they all lived in the same house, they'd have all the opportunity they needed.

THE MANSION WHERE the sisters and their father lived was searched. Nothing out of the ordinary was found.

Though, the police noted that it was possible the housekeepers had accidentally cleaned and thrown away any evidence. They mentioned the place, including the room where the father had passed away, was spotless.

Interesting. I flipped through to see what the housekeepers had to say. None of them had been in that room the day of the murder. They'd only seen Nia go in and out. She'd said that her father wasn't feeling well and didn't want to be disturbed.

"How about that?"

George grunted from his bed.

Oddly, not a single report pointed the finger at Nia.

I read it a bit further and understood. The Houston police were certain that Jasmine had something to do it with it. Probably because all of the sisters, and cousins, had given them Jasmine's name when asked if they thought anyone might want to harm the father.

But there was no evidence to support this theory. My

guess is that not a single one of them knew she'd been making amends, at least over the phone.

An uncomfortable feeling came over me. We had the dad's will, but we didn't really have any proof that Jasmine had actually been talking to her dad.

"No. I refuse to think like that. Besides, she didn't have access to her father." I shoved those thoughts out of my head.

It was a coincidence that Nia died in Jasmine's room. Her sister had surprised her with that visit. It took a lot of planning to poison someone. It all happened too quickly for it to be Jasmine.

Ugh. Reading these reports just gave me another headache. This case was so confusing. And from what I saw on the pages, the police in Houston and Sweet River had the same problem.

I called Kane and he answered on the first ring.

"Hey, we just stopped by your booth, and were wondering where you were," he said.

"Oh, is Eva with you?" That was Kane's girlfriend. They'd hit a bit of a rough patch over the holidays, but things seemed to be going well for them at the moment.

"Um. No. Jake and I showed up at your booth at the same time. Where are you?"

"I'm at the station waiting for Greg."

"Uh. Oh. Are you in trouble again?"

"Ha-ha. No, I'm actually here to share some information on Nia's case. I did have a question or two for you."

He sighed. "You know I can't discuss ongoing cases with you, unless Greg approves it."

"I could just break into your office. I've done it before."

He chuckled. "True."

"And you promised last time that as long as I shared with you what I'd discovered, you didn't mind letting me know what was going on."

"Yeah, but those were cases involving your friends. You don't know the people involved in this one."

I cleared my throat. "I do. Jasmine, one of the sisters, and I have become great friends. Whatever I can do to help her, I will."

"I see. What is it you want to know?"

"Cause of death for her father?"

"Well, the father, according to the medical examiner, died of a heart attack," Kane said.

"Oh. Then he wasn't murdered?"

"That was the initial cause of death. When I raised your concerns, they did a more thorough tox screening. It was almost too late, but they found faint traces of cyanide, which can mimic a heart attack. They didn't check for any poisons because he'd had two previous heart attacks and there was no suggestion of foul play."

Poison. I knew it. "Was it the same poison that killed Nia? And did she have any long-term illnesses?"

"Why are you asking me that?"

"I think someone was gas-lighting Nia and poisoning her father. Jasmine stayed in the house just one night and had the same sort of experiences that Nia did."

"Interesting. The poisoning for him was done slowly. So much so, that until the cyanide built up in his system, and looked like the flu, he didn't realize he was ill.

"He refused to see a doctor, but was bedridden for at least a week before he died. Everyone thought he had a bad virus, but since he wouldn't see a doctor—no one suspected foul play until the report came out that he'd died from cyanide. It's a very specific kind of rat poison. They don't even make that stuff anymore. But it was popular a century ago."

"And Nia?"

"Your brother is going to kill me. You did not hear any of this information from me."

"Pinkie swear."

He chuckled.

"Her heart was not in good shape. She had the same heart condition her father did."

"But they didn't die by the same poison?"

"Unfortunately, we only found death cap mushrooms in her system."

"What? And those killed her?"

"Yes. From what we can tell there is about a five- to six-hour span from when she ingested them, to when she died. Time of death is never one hundred percent accurate, unless there is a witness. So, that's an approximation."

"Where do you get those kinds of mushrooms?"

"They are usually hard to come by. Mostly, found in Europe. Though they've made a migration to the States. Houston is humid, so they grow fairly easily there. But it would take someone who really knew about that sort of stuff."

"Can I ask you a kind of crazy question?"

"You're going to do it anyway, so sure."

"Do you think there's a possibility it could be two different killers?"

He paused so long, I thought maybe the call had dropped.

"Kane?"

"I'm here. Maybe. Anything is possible at this point. These are two unusual deaths. Greg and the Houston police have been trying to sort it out for days. The dad was a prominent businessmen, and someone wants heads to roll for this."

"Thanks, and I promise not to say a word. That is…"

"If I promise to tell you if any new info comes in?"

I laughed. "Yes, sir. That's exactly what I was going to say."

We hung up. I flipped through more of the statements, but nothing stuck out at me. Except that they all blamed Jasmine. Which is weird, since the sisters had said they didn't know she'd moved back to Houston.

There were voices out in the lobby. I stacked everything just the way I found it, and ran around to the other side of the desk.

"Why didn't you answer your phone?" Greg asked.

Ooops. I hadn't noticed he'd called. "I was talking to a friend. Is everything okay?"

"Yep. There was a scuffle between Ms. Helen and Ms. Erma out at Mr. Green's general store. Seems Ms. Erma took the last can of some coffee they both like, and Ms. Helen pushed a cart into her. She swears it was an accident, but I'm not so sure about that."

Those two were the biggest gossips in town and knew

everything almost before it happened. They'd helped me more than once on a case.

"Did they brawl or something?"

He chuckled. "Ms. Erma refused to press charges, even though the cart did bruise her new hip. She said she'd put half the coffee in an airtight container to share. But that Ms. Helen owed her a dinner at the steakhouse and two boxes of chocolates.

"They'd already decided all of that before I even showed up. It's not like I have a festival to look out for, best man duties for Mike, or handling the shenanigans of college students who think love means writing things on the water tower."

I tried not to smile but I couldn't help it. "I saw that when I was driving in. It might have helped their cause if they'd added a name. Like, *I love you, Greg.*"

He smirked.

"So, why did you want to talk to me?"

He leaned back and crossed his arms. That meant he was mad at me about something.

"I heard you went to the memorial in Houston. And stayed overnight in the home of one of our suspects."

I rolled my eyes. "You heard, because I told you I was going. Remember, when I asked if you could watch George for me? But you were too busy?"

He frowned. "I only remember the part about the dog-sitting."

George grunted.

Greg smiled. "Of course, buddy, if I hadn't been on call, I absolutely wouldn't have minded."

"And Lucy already cleared Jasmine, who is as surprised by all of this as the rest of us."

"May I remind you that you've almost died twice because you trusted the wrong people?"

He was right.

"But this is different. Look, her family, keeps saying they didn't even know she was back in Houston. I was there, when they visited Jasmine at the B&B. There was genuine surprise on their faces.

"Though, I guess they could have been faking. I was also just half a block down when Jasmine was surprised by Nia. She had no idea she'd be there. And poison takes planning. Did you check their phone records?"

"Yes."

"And was there anything incriminating?" Sometimes it was like pulling teeth trying to get info from my brother.

He uncrossed his arms. "I don't suppose you remember the part where I told you to stay away from this. There is a lot of money involved, and you know that makes things more dangerous."

"Right. So, there weren't any calls between the sisters and Jasmine, right?"

He sighed, and then ran a hand through his hair. "No. It looks like the only phone calls between Jasmine and her family were a couple her dad made to her. And we know from his lawyer, that he was trying to make amends with her. Nia did try to contact her the night she died. But the calls went to voicemail."

"I think Nia knew someone was trying to kill her. I have this theory that she was coming to talk to Jasmine about it."

"Why don't you tell me everything you know," he said. "And I'll share what I can. Like, why do you think that about Nia?"

I told him about the family's reactions. And that Nia had been talking gibberish.

"Did she actually say, she found out too late?"

"Yes. Jasmine remembered it the other day. And I think the sister was poisoned before she even arrived."

"Could be," he said. "But then that means someone else would have had to know about the will, and you just said no one knew."

"Well, that's what the lawyer said. But if Nia found out, then someone else could have, right?"

He nodded. "Tell me again about the reaction to the video. What was your take?"

"You should have seen their heads turn when the dad said that he was leaving almost everything to Jasmine—and the whole place gasped.

"Jasmine had her head down. She couldn't believe it and she didn't want anything to do with any of that. I know I've made mistakes in the past by getting too close to suspects, but Jasmine—she's so much like Shannon and me, it's scary. It's like we've been friends forever."

"Kane says that Nia's liver and heart would have probably given out on her in the next year or so. They didn't find cyanide in her system, but maybe she figured out someone wanted her dead."

"I read that in the report. So what did you find out about the will?"

I explained everything, and then showed him the picture

from the datebook. "It could mean anything, but maybe she suspected one of them was trying to kill her."

"That's a good lead, especially since they had motive and opportunity."

"Well, motive if they knew about the will. That's the thing I can't figure out. They were all so surprised when the father announced that on the video."

"This case makes my head hurt," he said.

"Right there with you."

"You've found out more info in two days than I've been able to get from Houston in the last week. I sent Lucy back down there to investigate."

"So, if you had to guess, who do you think the killer or killers might be?"

"Excuse me. I need to faint. My brother just asked my opinions on a case."

He rolled his eyes.

"The sisters have been living under their dad's very strict thumb for years," I said. "From what I gathered it was an incredibly dysfunctional house. That might be enough to drive anyone to kill. They seem like nice enough people, but once her father announced who inherited the kingdom, there were actual hisses from her family.

"And she mentioned that she felt like she was in the car with a nest of vipers. It's why she hitched a ride with Shannon and me.

"Think about it. They've put up with their father all those years, and then he gave the keys to the kingdom to the sister who had run away. I'm more worried about one of them trying to kill Jasmine. You're always talking to me about motive, but Jasmine didn't really have one. Her sisters certainly did though."

He nodded. I hoped he was coming around to my way of thinking.

An idea hit me on the head like a big heavy rock. "There's one thing—it would put my mind at ease."

"We're all here for you, Ains." He smiled when he said it.

This time I was the one who did the eye roll. "Hey, have I not given you some good insider info?"

"Yes. So what is it you want to know?" Greg asked.

"We need to search Nia's computer and her bedroom more thoroughly," I said. "The police there might have missed something. Like, had she ever researched poisons?"

"You think she killed the father?"

"It's possible. Hardly anyone ever deletes their search history on their own laptop. I think it's worth looking into. If she was poisoning her father, there has to be evidence."

"It's plausible," Greg said.

"The will was made when Jasmine graduated college. What if Nia found out, and was so angry she killed her dad. Though, I remember the lawyer saying he was the only one with a copy of the will, as her father didn't want anyone else seeing it. Or maybe the sisters are all in it together?"

He smirked. "You're right. Unless the dad mentioned in one of their calls that he was giving it all to Jasmine, there's no way she could have known."

I sighed. "Greg, I was with her. She didn't have a clue. She was trembling and crying, and so confused. She even mentioned that when she was at the house she heard the voices. That's one of the reasons she didn't go back after the funeral."

Greg rubbed the bridge of his nose with his fingers.

Then it hit me. I pulled out my phone.

"Who are you calling?"

I held up a hand.

"Ainsley? Hey, how are you?"

"I'm great. I was just checking up on you."

"I've spent a great deal of time with the lawyers and my uncle. It's been a crazy day."

"I can't even imagine everything you're going through. Oh, I just thought of something I wanted to ask you."

"Anything, I'm not sure what I would have done without you and Shannon."

"You mentioned that you heard voices in Nia's room."

There was a long pause.

"I promise, it's for a good reason. Do you remember drinking or eating anything that might have been weird or made you uncomfortable?"

"No. I told you that I was so overwhelmed, just being in the house. I'm having a tough time remembering any of that. Like, maybe I imagined the voices?"

"I don't think you did."

Greg cocked his head.

"Did you eat or drink anything right before you went to bed?"

"Tea. Nia had one of those instant tea makers, and there was one that smelled like cinnamon and apples. But it had a real earthy taste, and I only took a few sips."

"Okay. Remember when I said we should probably get

you to a doctor to see if maybe someone gave you something?"

"Yes," she said hesitantly.

"I want you to go to the emergency room now. Tell them you may have been accidentally poisoned. I'm going to call the coroner here, to see if he can work some magic to get your blood tested quickly."

There was a sob. "Do you think it's killing me? I do have a horrible headache, but I thought it was from all this paperwork."

"I'm betting if you only took a few sips, you're fine. That may be why you thought you saw Nia. There might have been some sort of hallucinogen in the tea."

"Okay. I wish you lived closer."

"I know. If I didn't have to teach tomorrow, I'd be there. I mean, if you want to come here, if you feel like driving, we can get Kane to test you."

She didn't say anything.

"Jasmine?"

"I'm here."

"Are you okay?"

"Yes. Except for the headache I feel fine. The press is outside the building and if I go to the hospital here, they'll follow. And there will be even more gossip about my family."

"Right, but we need to make sure you are okay." I was genuinely worried and furious that I'd forgotten to get her checked out.

"I just realized I have three helicopters at my disposal now. It's weird, right? I'm not sure I'll ever get used to this."

Greg was writing quickly on a pad of paper. Then he

shoved it my way. It was an address for the old hangar outside of town. Private planes, for people who owned the ranches around here, flew in and out of there all the time.

"If you want to keep it private, you could come here." I gave her the information. "And you are welcome to stay with me," I said.

Greg shook his head.

"I've just booked a room at Mrs. Carmichael's. I was planning on coming to the Valentine's Day dance. She's been so sweet and she sent me an email last night, saying if I needed to hang out at the B&B to get away from everyone, that her door was always open.

"And you've scared me to death, so now I'm afraid to even be here in my apartment. Oh, the pilot just texted back. He'll be here in ten minutes and he says it's a short flight. I'll be there soon. Ainsley?"

"Yes."

"If anything happens to me. Please find out who is doing all of this."

"You're going to be fine," I said firmly. I think maybe more to convince myself.

"Thank you."

"No worries."

After I hung up, Greg snorted.

"What?"

"She genuinely likes you."

I gave him the evil eye. "And why wouldn't she? I'm kind of awesome."

He snorted again. "If you say so. You're right about one thing."

"Stop the presses!"

"She was genuinely scared she'd been poisoned. I've been a cop for a long time. I heard it in her voice."

"We were in my car when she told us that she'd heard the voices and seen her dead sister running down the hall. I remember thinking that I should take her to the hospital. But we got sidetracked."

He leaned back in his chair again. "I'll call Houston and tell them to get another search warrant. We need to get our hands on that tea."

I nodded.

My mind whirled with possibilities. I was so in my head that I was at the front door of the station, when my brother yelled, "Ainsley!" My heart beat so fast I thought I might die.

"Don't yell."

"Did you forget something?" He pointed at George who was sitting beside him. Maybe it was the sun coming through the door, but I swear my dog narrowed his eyes at me.

"Right. Sorry, he usually follows me."

That satisfied my brother, but George not so much. When I stepped outside, he sat down and refused to budge.

"Come on, buddy. I have a lot to do."

Still, he wouldn't move. I'd insulted him and he wasn't over the fact I'd left him for a few days.

"How about we go see if we can find the dog bakery lady. I think she has a booth at the festival."

He cocked his head and eyed me suspiciously.

"And if she isn't, I'll get treats from Shannon."

"Roh-ray," he said.

Or at least his grumbling sounded like *okay*.

"Who's a good dog?" I rubbed his head, and then hugged him. He rested his head on my shoulder and sighed. "Poor guy. Maybe we should get two treats."

Four seconds later, he pulled me down the street, nearly ripping my arm out of my shoulder socket.

We found the booth, thanks to George's very healthy nose. And then we took the treats back to the booth.

"You're alive!" Carrie cheered. "Sorry, I forgot to text you. We've been really busy."

There were quite a few people milling about the booth.

"No worries. As you can see, I survived. Do either of you need a break?"

They shook their heads. "We're good," Maria said. "It's such a beautiful day, it's fun to be outside."

"Okay. Text me if you need me. I'm going to walk around a bit." I gave George another treat and waited while he ate it.

We walked down a few booths, and something smelled like Christmas. It was a booth full of apothecary jars. Each of them had a different type of tea.

"This place smells amazing."

The woman, who was probably in her midthirties, smiled at me.

"Thank you. Herbs and aromatherapy can change a person's mood," she said. "Do you have favorite scents or tastes?"

I nodded. "I love cinnamon and cloves."

"Ahhh, you were drawn in by the orange spice I believe. Did it smell like Christmas?"

"Yes."

"It's this one. Would you like to try some?"

After finding out my friend's tea might have been poisoned, I was more than hesitant.

"When my children were younger, and needed antibiotics or medicines that didn't taste good, I always added a bit of this. The cloves, cinnamon, apples and oranges help hide the taste of bitter medicines."

Just what I'd been thinking. "Wait. You said when your kids were younger. How old are they now?"

She laughed. "Well, they're grown men now. But they will always be my babies. Let's see, the oldest is twenty-nine, and the youngest twenty-six."

"Wow. Did you have them when you were ten—sorry, that's rude. You just look so young."

She laughed. "Thank you. Again, it's the tea. This is the blend that keeps me young," she said as she pointed to a jar to her right. "It's my secret mix, so I won't share everything, but two of the biggest components are green tea and golden monkey. And I mix a bit of chaga, which is a mushroom that helps detox the body, and I throw a few adaptogens in."

"I feel like you're the best commercial for your products. I'd like to try that one."

"I sell by the ounce." She pointed to her sign. The green teas were slightly more expensive, but if it made my skin look like hers, I was all for it. Of course, I'd never heard of some of the things she was talking about. I'd have to research them.

I made the purchase and took her card that had her website on it. She'd mentioned it was best to drink it first thing in the morning.

After checking with my gang at the booth, who told me to just go home, I headed for my car. The last few days had been hectic and I was kind of tired. George was ready for a nap.

I opened the hatch to put the few things I'd bought in, and it hit me. If she was coming by helicopter, how would she get into town?

I texted and asked if she needed a ride.

No. Got it covered. I'll see you tomorrow. After the test, I'm crashing. Didn't sleep at all last night.

About that time, Greg's police SUV zoomed past on the side street.

"I wonder where he's going?"

I texted back: *Let me know how it goes and I'm here if you need me.*

I put George in and then sat down in the driver's seat.

A minty smell filled the car. "Wow, that tea is stronger than I thought. Do you think it really works? Or maybe it's just good genetics?"

George huffed and lay down in the back seat.

A few minutes later, I was pulling up in my driveway when I noticed something strange.

There was a man in a giant heart costume, standing on my porch.

Chapter Sixteen

THE ELDERLY GENTLEMAN in the heart costume held a boom box. I expected George to run up and do his you're-invading-my-territory bark, but he sat down at the first step and cocked his head, as if he were trying to figure out what was going on.

Right there with you, buddy.

"Can I help you?" Maybe he'd escaped from the assisted living center at the edge of town. About once every three months, there was an Amber Alert for the elderly around here. They were a bunch of escape artists.

"Are you Ainsley McGregor?"

How did he know my name? "Yes."

George and I stayed on the bottom step. I didn't want to startle the poor man; he was obviously lost.

"Got a song for you."

Then he pushed the button.

"Dear Ainsley, Thank you, for all you do. We don't know what we'd do without you. We love you." The warbly song went on, and I was fairly certain this poor man didn't know what vocal pitch was. But it made me smile.

George lay down on the ground and put his paws over his eyes. I had to laugh. I couldn't help it.

"…we wish you all the love… That's from the gang at

Bless Your Art. Have a good day."

Then he passed me on the porch and sauntered down my driveway, as if he didn't have a care in the world.

"I bet he's cold," I said to George. My dog glanced around and then sighed.

"That was something." I'd been in such shock I forgot to take a picture and I had a feeling no one would believe me.

Note to self: Not a fan of singing telegrams.

Though, I'd be laughing about that for years to come.

I texted the gang and thanked them, though, I hoped that wouldn't encourage them to ever do that again.

After letting George outside, I was about to heat something for dinner when my phone rang.

"Hey, Shannon, what's up?"

"Did you get one too?"

"What?"

"A singing telegram?"

"Oh, yes. It was—disturbing."

She laughed. "Mine was some old guy in a cupid costume. I can't believe Mike did that to me. Though, it's been a crazy day with all the tourists here for the festival, and it did make me laugh out loud."

"The team at Bless Your Art sent mine, so maybe Mike got the idea from them?"

"Probably. Did yours show up at the shop?"

"No, he was on my porch when I got home. I think George may be scarred for life."

She laughed again.

"Well, everyone getting their afternoon caffeine fixes witnessed mine. Funny thing is, Ms. Helen and Ms. Erma were at their regular table, and I swear they were swooning over him."

"I was worried about my guy getting hypothermia. He was eighty, if he was a day."

"Mike says it's guys from the veteran's club. They did it as a charity drive for the Wounded Vets."

"Awww. Now I feel bad for laughing."

"Don't. From what I understand, they sent out their oldest members because they wanted it to be funny. And I don't know about you, but I needed that."

We both chuckled. How sweet for those guys, most of whom had served their country and put their lives on the line for it, to do that for their fellow veterans. I made a note on the calendar by the door to send money to the charity in the Vet Hall's name.

"Oh. The main reason I was calling is did you see the news?"

"I just walked in the door. What happened?"

"Jasmine is missing, or at least, that's what the news reports are saying. Her face has been splashed all over the place. And there is a lot of speculation. I was worried about her."

That was strange. Her helicopter should have landed a few minutes ago.

"I just talked to her about an hour and half ago, and she was heading here. Hold on, I'm going to text her. Oh, wait she's calling me. Let me see if I can merge the calls."

"Ainsley?"

"Hi, Jasmine. You're on with me and Shannon. Are you okay?"

She laughed. "I am, now. Turns out, I'm not big on helicopter rides. I got really sick when we landed. But I'm fine now. Your friend Kane, or should we just call him Idris Elba—I mean, that man is hot—helped me. He's taken the blood samples. He and your brother were worried that maybe I'd been poisoned, so I'm still here in the hospital. They're going to keep me overnight."

"Oh no," Shannon said. "Tell us what you need."

"I'm good. Really. They promised to give me something to help me sleep. And I was dehydrated, so they've got an IV running. I'm drinking some broth and then asking for the sleeping pill."

"I don't blame you," I said. "But we're here for—"

"What in the world?" Jasmine screeched. "I'm not missing."

"I'm guessing you turned on the news," I said.

"Why would someone even think that? They're making it sound like I became a billionaire and then ran off somewhere with the family fortune. Ugh."

"What can we do to help?" I said. "I'm assuming, you don't want them to know you're in town?"

"Yes. Actually, I think I can take care of this with a statement from the company. I just need to call our marketing and publicity department. Though, I'm not sure what to say."

I flipped on the news but turned the volume down. "Maybe that you appreciate the concern but you are fine. That you are working with your team to make the transition as seamless as possible. And that you hope those concerned will respect your need to mourn in private during this difficult time."

"That's perfect, thank you. I keep saying this, but God putting you in my path is one of the best things that ever happened to me. I really don't know what I'd do without you. Listen, I should be back at the B&B tomorrow. Let's get lunch or dinner, whatever is easiest for you. And, Shannon, if there's something I can do to help with the wedding, let me know."

Shannon laughed. "It's not like you're taking over a multi-billion-dollar corporation," she said.

"True. But I welcome all distractions at the moment. Honestly, I've asked everyone to carry on, while I take some time to grieve for my father. And I am grieving, though it all feels so surreal. I get a daily rundown from the team, and so far, not much has changed except for the name of the CEO."

"Okay," Shannon said, "but I warn you: if you offer to help, I'll take you up on it. Actually, I was going to head out to the venue to see how the cleanup is going there. The facility hadn't been used since last fall, and it was pretty dusty. Do you guys want to go with me? I'll pack a picnic for tomorrow afternoon?"

We agreed and hung up.

Shannon called me back. "How did you know what to say?"

"Olivia Pope."

"Ohhhh. *Scandal*. I miss that show."

"Me, too. See you tomorrow."

Next, I called Kane.

"I don't have any results yet," he said. "They're doing a full blood profile at the hospital. I probably won't hear from the lab until tomorrow morning."

"Hi, how are you? I'm fine. Ainsley, was there something I could help you with?"

He chuckled. "Sorry, just really busy. That is why you were calling, right?"

"Well, yes. Thank you. Do you think she's safe in the hospital?"

"Greg put some of his men outside her door. He's erring on the side of caution. He doesn't want another murder of a Levy family member on his watch."

"Me either. Shannon and I have gotten really close to Jasmine."

"She's a nice lady and she's been through a lot," he said.

"So, will you unofficially let me know if you guys find anything out?"

There was a long pause. "If it will keep you from breaking into my office, yes."

I smiled.

I sat down on the couch with my notes from everything I'd gathered over the past few weeks. But then I remembered I hadn't uploaded my teaching videos for my classes. The college where I taught part-time had moved my classes online.

I'd been accidentally shot by a suspect in a case in December, and wasn't quite ready to go back to work at the school on the first of January. Well, I was, but the doctor wouldn't give me a release. The dean had wanted to do more remote learning, and my classes are popular, so she set it up.

It was actually easier for me, because I could check in anytime. But I missed the face-to-face interaction with my students. Luckily, I had two students from former classes, Lily and Jeff, who helped me keep track of assignments and tutored some of the kids who needed extra help.

Once I finished all of that, I stared at my notebook. The big whiteboard where I usually put my notes was at the store. I'm a visual person—it's why I love art so much—and I needed to see things a certain way.

Then I noticed the sticky note app on my computer.

"This might just work."

Two hours later, I had narrowed down my list of suspects. I needed to talk to all of them. But I wasn't sure how I could do that since they lived in Houston.

The main players were the sisters, uncle and cousin. I could see why someone might want the father dead. It didn't make it right, but years of living under that sort of dictator, who ruled over every aspect of their lives, had to create resistance and resentment.

But why kill Nia? The sisters loved her. The uncle and cousin did as well. As much as I hated to say it, it made more sense for the killer to go after Jasmine. She was the usurper.

I have to stop watching *Game of Thrones* reruns.

None them had to worry about money.

But what if it wasn't just about the money?

Even though the uncle seemed nice enough, he'd been running the company while the dad was ill. Maybe he wasn't as excited about Jasmine being in charge as he pretended to be. It wouldn't be the first time a fight for power and control ended in a murder. But how did he poison the tea in Nia's room? Well, if that's what happened. Why couldn't all these lab techs be as concerned as I was? I needed answers.

"This is hurting my brain," I said, as I closed the notebook.

"What is?" Jake's voice boomed from the kitchen.

I may have accidentally tossed my laptop to the floor and screeched.

"When did you come in?"

We had keys to each other's places, so we seldom knocked.

He carried two plates of lasagna to the coffee table and set them down. Then, he picked up my laptop and carefully sat it on one of the side tables.

"You were working so intensely, I didn't want to bother you. We made lasagna at the firehouse tonight and I thought you might want some."

"Always." I smiled. And then he leaned down for a kiss. Jake's lips—let's just say, they were poem-worthy. His touch, even if he was just holding my hand, sent warmth through me.

"So, what was hurting your head?"

Jake and I made a promise a few months ago to always tell the truth, even if the other person might not like what they hear.

I pursed my lips. "Well, I don't know if you heard, but my new friend Jasmine is in the hospital."

"Is she okay?"

"They ran some blood tests here in Sweet River and are watching her overnight."

"I'm sure she'll be fine, but I'm sorry you're worried."

Have I mentioned how sweet he is?

"I have been making notes of conversations I've overheard or stories that the sisters were telling the other day. The thing that's tough, is that they all seem like pretty decent people."

"I guess Greg telling you to stay out of it, is never going to work?"

We laughed. "Look, I didn't meant to make best friends with a billionaire and get access to her possibly murderous family; it just happened."

"I'm just glad you're telling me. So in this soap opera, who has the most to gain?"

"That's just it. No one is walking away poor. I can't figure out if it's about power, and running the company? Or if Nia and her dad did something that really made someone angry. The police in Houston don't really have anything. And until recently, Greg and his guys thought the prime suspect was Jasmine."

"Hmm. Let's eat our lasagna and give your brain a rest. Then you can take me through it step by step."

"Really?"

He nodded. "You're good at this and I don't mind being your sounding board."

"You're awesome. Wait, I thought you were on duty tonight?"

"I am. But it's slow, so I thought I'd come check on you. I heard the weirdest rumor about you."

"Oh?"

"That some guy was singing to you on your porch? Should I be worried?"

"Oh, hon, that is not a rumor, and yes, you should most definitely be worried." I winked and then we laughed.

"Did you lose your keys again?" he asked.

"No. Why? And I don't lose my keys. They just like to play hide-and-seek at least once a week."

He chuckled. "I just noticed your lock on the back door looks like it has scratches around it. I thought maybe you tried to use a screwdriver to get in."

"That's strange. Oh, it might have been George. When I don't get up and answer the door right away, he starts pawing at it."

Jake pursed his lips. "Maybe, that's it. George, did you scratch the back door?"

My dog was napping on his end of the couch. He opened one eye, closed it and then rolled onto his back sticking his long legs straight in the air.

It was so funny, I almost snorted the water I'd been drinking through my nose.

"Is he playing dead?"

"His version of it," I answered.

"So guilty as charged?"

"Probably."

"Good. I was worried maybe someone had tried to break in."

Ugh. Why did he have to go and say that? But I didn't want him to worry, and he would if I said something.

"Nah. Just the hairy beast with the giant paws. I'm lucky the inside of the door doesn't look like that."

But I was sticking my nose into something where it didn't really belong. Was someone mad about that?

If they were, it meant I was probably onto something.

Chapter Seventeen

THE NEXT DAY, the drive out to the Old Barn—that was the name of the place—was a gorgeous one. The road was lined with pine trees that were lit throughout the year with white lights. It was almost five, and just before we arrived at the barn, all of the lights popped on the trees.

"I can see why you chose this place," Jasmine said. "It's gorgeous."

"Please, tell that to my mother. She's so upset I'm not getting married in a church. But we may have found a way around that."

"How?" I asked. That had been the only hitch in the wedding plans. Shannon and Mike loved nature. They'd considered having an outdoor wedding, but this time of year, the weather was iffy at best. The Barn was the next best thing. It was in the middle of a pine forest and sat on a cliff above a riverbank. It was rustic but beautiful.

"Father Brown came and blessed the barn and the acreage around it. So, technically, it's sacred ground. And he's letting us borrow the lighted cross the church uses at Christmas to put outside."

"That's so smart. Good for you guys and Father Brown," I said.

Shannon opened the double doors. While the outside

was painted navy with white trim, the inside was natural and white-painted wood. When Shannon flipped the light switch, we gasped. The rafters arched gracefully at the top, and rows of painted white chairs sat in several rows.

"This is gorgeous," Jasmine whispered.

There were twinkle lights on ficus trees all the way down the aisle. It was beautiful in a simple way, and very Shannon.

"Ainsley, when you came out we couldn't get inside, so what do you think?"

"It's perfect." My eyes watered a little.

"Oh. No. Don't cry," Shannon said. "I'm this close to blubbering like a baby."

"Me too," said Jasmine.

"I'm just so happy for you guys." I hugged Shannon. "Do not let anyone take this joy from you. Not your mom, or anyone else. And if they try, tell me, I will sic George on them."

We all laughed.

Shannon sighed happily. "That you guys get why this is the place really means a lot to me. I'm so excited. Now, let me show you what we're thinking for the altar."

She opened her giant notebook and pointed at some rose-covered arches. "The only thing I'm sad about is we can't use real flowers. Mike's mom and sisters have terrible allergies, so, yep. It's not ideal, but it can't be helped. I don't want them sneezing through the ceremony."

I smiled. "And you can reuse the flowers when you do weddings at the winery."

"Oh, that's a great idea. Any wedding in particular? Did Jake ask you the big question?"

"Jake?" Jasmine asked.

"Have you not met him? That's Ainsley's boyfriend. He looks like a dark-haired Chris Hemsworth."

"Oh. My. Do all the men in this town look like celebrities?"

"Yes," Shannon and I said at the same time.

"And no," I said. "We've never discussed marriage."

Jake didn't like to talk about relationship stuff, and I wasn't super comfortable with it. And we'd only been dating seriously for a short while. It wasn't time yet.

"Hmmm," Shannon said.

"What?" I asked.

"I'm going to get into big trouble if I say something and it doesn't happen. So, I should keep my mouth shut," Shannon said. "Uh. Let me show you where the reception is being held."

"Hey, wait a minute. You don't get away that easily," I said.

"What she said," Jasmine joked. "I want to know what that hmmm meant just as much as you do."

Shannon opened another door and flipped on the lights. A cloud of dust whooshed around us.

"Ugh." Shannon coughed. "I guess they haven't cleaned in here yet. Basically, we're going to do an oval with the tables, so that everyone feels a part of it. I never like being stuck in the back by the restrooms. That's where a lot of singles have to sit. And we have a lot of older folks, and I want them to feel a part of things."

The tables and chairs were stacked against the walls. But this room had the beautiful arched rafters as well, and it would be beautiful once it was decorated.

"You are such a kind heart," Jasmine said. "After everything—well, I feel like you two were put in my path so I could remember there are fair and decent people with good hearts in the world."

"Awww." Shannon hugged Jasmine. "We are always here for you, friend. And I know you're super busy, but I'd love for you to be a part of our celebration."

"Are you sure?"

Shannon nodded.

"I'd love to come. Thank you both for making me feel so welcome. Oh. You need to tell Ainsley why you said hmmm. I'm dying to know."

"Just don't—I don't want you to get your hopes up, Ainsley."

I had no idea what she was talking about.

"Okay. I pretty much go into every situation expecting the worst. Just tell me."

"Well, Mike said that Jake asked him where he got my engagement ring."

"Oh." I wasn't sure what to say. "I don't think it's that. Maybe he's shopping for something for his mom."

The two women stared at me like I was crazy. "What? He's close to his mom and his sister. Valentine's Day is coming up. Ya know. Could be anything."

Because if he were going to ask me to marry him, wouldn't he say something? Or at least hint at it?

"Sure," Shannon said. "He's shopping for his mom. Well, that's the end of the tour. I do want to come put final touches on the day before the rehearsal, so I'll need your help that day, Ains."

"No problem."

"I'll help, too," said Jasmine. "Oh, and if you need candles, I can do some tapered ones that have the love juju in them. That's a great start to a happy marriage, and the aroma will make everyone feel in a loving way toward you and your husband."

"Oh, I'd love that. If it's not too much trouble."

She shook her head. "I will have to go home in a few days for supplies. I'll see if I can get back in time."

After locking up the barn, we headed to the car. The temperature had dropped since the sun had gone down. We climbed into the SUV but it wouldn't start—as in dead as a doornail.

"Oh. No," Shannon said.

"It's probably just cold," I said. It was fairly new and I'd never had any trouble with it. I waited a few seconds and tried again. Nothing.

"Let me call Mike," Shannon said. "He's really good with cars… Or not." She shook her phone. "No bars. Crud. I just remembered it was one of the reasons we liked it out here. No chance of someone's cell phone disturbing the ceremony."

"I don't usually panic but I'm kind of nervous," Jasmine said. "Should we try to walk back?"

I shook my head. "It's a long walk. Let me pop the hood and see if I can figure it out." I grabbed a flashlight. I stared at the engine as if I had the power to turn it over with my eyes.

Shannon and Jasmine joined me.

"Try jiggling the thingies on top of the battery. Sometimes they come loose. That happened with my old car."

I checked the connections but everything seemed to be on tight. "Any other ideas?"

"Uh." Jasmine had a weird look on her face. "Maybe this is supposed to be connected to something?" She held up a cable that was split in two.

"That doesn't look good," I said. "It's so weird. I just went in for my six-month car check. I'm kind of OCD about it."

Shannon took one of the cables. "Ains, shine your light on this."

I did as she asked.

"Is it just me, or does this look like a clean cut? Like maybe someone did it with a knife?" Shannon asked.

We looked at each other and the woods surrounding us.

I shivered.

Shannon's hand shook, and Jasmine turned in circles as if she were looking for an intruder.

"Right. So. We're stuck. For now," I said. I was surprised by how calm I sounded. What if someone was out there in the woods? No one would find our bodies for days.

"What should we do?" Jasmine asked. Her voice trembled. "Do you think someone wants to hurt us?"

I sighed. "I hope not. But it's probably best if we get somewhere behind a locked door."

"I still have the picnic," Shannon said. Since it had been chilly, we decided after we went to the venue, that we'd go back to my place and have girls' night.

"And we can go back inside and turn the heat on in the

barn," Shannon added. "There's a full kitchen there. We'll just hang out until help comes. Or, if no one shows up by morning… we'll try to make the walk. And um, we'll be behind doors that lock."

Jasmine glanced out at the woods again. "I'm great with whatever you two want to do, as long as it's inside."

AFTER TWO BOTTLES of wine, and enough food to feed an army, we were all yawning. Shannon had pulled some old tablecloths out of the linen closet. And we put some folding tables together for temporary beds.

We talked until, eventually, the other two fell asleep.

Even though I was drowsy from the wine, I couldn't relax and it had nothing to do with the hard table I was lying on.

Two questions rolled around in my brain.

Who cut my battery cable? And why?

But it was a third question that kept me awake. I shivered and glanced out of the windows.

Are they still here?

Just then a shadowy figure passed by the window.

"Wake up." I may have screamed a little. "Someone is outside."

Shannon and Jasmine sat straight up.

"What's wrong?" Shannon asked.

"Someone is outside," I said, a bit more quietly this time.

"Oh no," Shannon said. "We need weapons." She ran for the knife block on the counter. After carefully handing me a large butcher knife, she took two for herself, and Jasmine did the same.

"What do we do now?" Jasmine said. Her voice wasn't nearly as nervous as mine.

"Maybe, I should go outside and check on things."

"No!" they shouted in unison.

"Have you never seen a horror movie?" Shannon asked. "That's how the killer picks us off one by one. And I refuse to die before my wedding."

"She's right," Jasmine added. "We need to stick together and stay behind closed doors. It's always the idiots who go down into the dark basement who end up dead. Also, the black girl is always the first to go, so we stay together."

I was just trying to be brave, but I had no real desire to go outside. "Let's double-check all of the locks."

We did that, and then stood in the middle of the kitchen.

"It's been a long time since I've been this scared," Shannon said. "Well, except that time when someone cut your brake lines."

Jasmine snorted and I couldn't help but smile. "So it's not just my fault? This sort of thing happens to you a lot?"

"Unfortunately," I said. "Strange things have been happening out at my ranch, so it might not even be related."

"You didn't tell me that," Shannon said.

I shrugged. "I thought it was kids messing around, but now, I'm not so sure."

There was a strange sound and we all froze.

"Thunder," I whispered. There were sighs of relief. Then rain poured down in buckets. "Well, if they are still out there, they're getting wet."

"Serves them right," Shannon said. "I wish someone would realize we haven't come back yet."

"Me too."

"I don't know about you two, but I could use some more wine," Shannon said. "My nerves are a mess."

"I second that," Jasmine said.

I went along with them, but I didn't drink more than a few sips. There was no way I'd let my guard down.

Someone was out there, and I was determined they wouldn't hurt my friends.

I'D BEEN STARING at the kitchen door for what seemed like forever. Sleep tried to take over, but I stood up and walked around the kitchen.

I jumped when a siren blared.

"What the—" Jasmine said sleepily.

There was a loud banging on the barn door.

"Ainsley? Are you okay?" Jake sounded very worried.

"We're okay. Hold on, Shannon's unlocking the door."

As soon as she turned the knob, he rushed inside and wrapped his arms around me.

"We've been worried sick," he said, squeezing me so tight, I couldn't breathe. He was warm and smelled like pine trees. "What happened?"

"We think someone cut my—" My mind was so fuzzy, I couldn't think.

"Battery cable," Jasmine offered.

I lifted my head off Jake's shoulder. "Oh, this is Jasmine."

Jake, ever the gentleman, let go of me to shake her hand.

"Why would someone do that?" Jake asked.

I shrugged. "Your guess is as good as mine."

He frowned and then looked at Jasmine. She held up her hands in surrender.

I slapped his chest lightly. "She was with us, silly. Though, it's possible someone is following her. We came to see what Shannon had planned for the wedding. Oh, how did you know where we were?"

"Mike said you were doing wedding stuff, but he had no idea where you were. He and Greg are searching your place, the coffee shop and your store."

"But how did you find me?"

"We were coming back from some training and your find my friend app dinged as we drove past."

"But we didn't have bars on our phones."

Shannon groaned. "I'm so dumb."

"What?" Jasmine and I said at the same time.

"There is internet here. It's weak. But they have it in the office so photographers can upload their stuff to the cloud when necessary. We couldn't call but we could have texted them."

I started laughing and then Jasmine, and then Shannon did. We were laughing so hard, I nearly fell down.

Jake and his men gave us strange looks, which only made us laugh harder.

"I think we better get you home," Jake said. "It's late. I'll have a tow truck bring your car in."

When we walked outside, it was still pitch black. "What time is it?"

"Nine?"

The girls and I started laughing again.

"It's only been five hours."

Shannon started singing a little song. "We are the mountain women, survivors we are strong."

"Sir, do you think they are delirious?" one of the men asked Jake.

"Ainsley, any chance there was wine consumed tonight?"

I made the universal sign for a little bit.

"Nope, they're fine," Jake said. "Let's get them home."

By the time they dropped us all off, it was all I could do to keep my eyes open. Jake helped me upstairs. He took off my boots, and then pulled the covers up over me.

"I love you," I said.

"I love you, too. Hold on. Don't fall asleep yet."

He ran downstairs, and then came back up with a glass and some ibuprofen. "Drink this now," he said. Then helped me sit up.

I drank several gulps.

"Now take these." He put two tablets in my hands. My head already hurt, so I was grateful for the meds.

I was so sleepy, I could barely keep my eyes open.

"Good. Now get some rest."

He was at the doorway when he stopped and turned back.

We smiled at one another.

"Hey, Jake?"

"Yes?"

"Why would someone cut the battery cable in the middle of nowhere? And maybe it wasn't George."

It worried me that maybe someone was trying to get to Jasmine through me.

"George? What do you mean?"

"The scratched door. I looked this morning—it wasn't him."

He frowned.

"I wonder if someone is trying to kill me again."

Chapter Eighteen

THE LAST DAY of the festival culminated in a big Valentine's Day dance at the community center. After work, school, and trying to figure out who sabotaged my car, I wanted nothing more than to curl up on my couch and sleep a day or three. But Bless Your Art was the charity sponsor for the auction and I had to be there.

Unfortunately, Jake had to work. Though, he'd been making up for that over the past week by doing small things around my house, or dropping flowers by. And every morning I'd wake up to find him passed out on my couch. He was worried that someone had tried to break in the other night.

Greg and his team had been out to check my door and property, but other than knowing the scratches were made by a screwdriver, which I'd figured out on my own, they didn't have any other clues.

And there was no reason for anyone to come after me—unless they were trying to get to Jasmine. But none of it made sense.

Neither did the case of her sister and father's murders.

Jake had asked Mike and Shannon to take me to the dance, but I'd let Shannon know that I wanted to drive my car so I could skip out right after the auction.

I'd never had a man be so attentive toward me, and that

it was Jake made it all the more special.

George and I had just walked in the door at home when my cell rang.

"Hey, Kane, what's up?"

"Well, your idea to have them search Nia's room paid off. Her tea and coffee maker had traces of the cyanide found in her father's bloodstream."

So, Nia was the one who killed her father. Wow. I guess in a way, I'd sort of suspected it but I thought it a bit odd that the machine was in her bathroom. After he died, why wouldn't she get rid of the evidence?

"So, Nia killed him?"

"Yes," he said.

"Someone could have moved the machine in there, after they were both dead. To throw off suspicion," I said.

"Yep. Since she didn't die there, no one had thought to do a thorough CSI of her room. But it was extremely clean. And traces of the same sort of poison were in Jasmine's blood, though not enough to hurt her. She's lucky she didn't drink more of the tea."

"Hmmm. Then all we need to know is who killed her?"

"Do you have any theories?" he asked.

"That's a first."

"What?"

"That you're asking me what I think. You and Greg usually just tell me to stay out of things."

"Well, you do have a habit of nearly getting yourself killed. But you do have a quick mind and a knack for finding murderers. So, do you have any theories?"

"I don't know. We're talking about two different killers

here. It makes sense that Nia was tired of her father's behavior. It doesn't excuse her, but the motive is clear. If she wasn't ingesting the cyanide, what was making Nia talk gibberish and act strangely? Her sisters said she'd been acting weird."

Unless the sisters were lying. Perhaps, to make it look like their crazy sister killed their dad. Ugh. This case was so frustrating.

"I'm not sure how, but I think Nia found out about her father's will. She had to be absolutely furious. She'd been his number two for years.

"Then he gives the company to the daughter, who she believed, gave up on the family and makes her share the responsibility of running it with Jasmine. The one person who never wanted anything to do with the empire. That would be enough to drive anyone mad, especially given her father's behavior all these years. Oh, did you look at her brain?"

"We did. We didn't see anything."

"Right. But if she wasn't thinking clearly—how did she actually find Jasmine? They hadn't seen or talked to each other in ten years, at least."

"And the records on both their phones show no contact at all," Kane said. "Except for some that went straight to voice mail the night the victim died. I need to know where those death cap mushrooms came from."

I typed Jasmine's name into the search bar. Tons of recent articles came up, but at the top of all that was the site for her candle business. I clicked on it, and there was a link to places where she was doing events, and where her candles were sold. My store was there, and she had Sweet River listed to sell her stuff at the festival.

"I know how Nia found Jasmine. It said she'd be here for the festival, and that she was excited about selling her wares in Bless Your Art. She wrote a blog post about it. Nia must have figured since it was a new post, she might still be here."

"Okay, but where do the mushrooms come in?"

That I didn't know. "What if she got them on the internet or something and she was going to poison Jasmine? I mean, with her sister out of the way, it would be easier for her to take control of the company. And maybe she touched them, and they killed her? Is that possible?"

Kane was quiet for a minute.

"Did I lose you?"

"I'm here. I'm looking up the levels of the toxins. Just a little bit will kill you. Oh, yeah. No, with the levels I'm seeing, she would have had to ingest them."

"Okay. How long does it take for the poison to work?"

"It depends on the person. But my guess is within a few hours. Like I told you before, time of death is approximate."

"Do you know if the police have any idea where Nia was before she drove to Sweet River?"

"Let me look."

"That's interesting. There is about a four-hour gap from when she left the office, until she got here. No one knows where she was. The office said she had only come in for a few hours. She left for lunch and didn't come back. Her assistant said she had dinner plans but it doesn't say with who. And I'm not seeing any follow-up on that."

I'd be making a call to the assistant in a bit.

"At most, it's an hour-and-a-half drive from her office to here."

"But we know she didn't get here until about eight forty-five. That's when the bank security cameras clocked her coming into town. I remember Greg mentioning it when I was working on time of death. And then the security cameras at the edge of the park, clocked her parallel parking at 8:47."

"We finished dinner at Dooley's around nine, and I saw the sister approach her. Well, I didn't actually see Nia. Jasmine stopped and it looked like she was talking to someone."

"This is interesting."

"What?"

"I'm looking through some studies of cases. Depending on the amount ingested, it can take three to five days for organ failure."

"But she had a heart condition, right?"

"Yes, which made her more susceptible than most to the poison."

"Okay, so we need to know everywhere Nia went, I'd say for a twenty-four-hour period."

"I honestly think you can shorten that to ten hours," he said. "I need time to run some numbers. I may be able to work out just how long it took to kill her, given the contents in her stomach, her tox levels, and general health."

"Okay. Great. But after the dance, okay? I don't want Eva killing me for making you miss it."

"About that. Eva and I broke up again."

"Oh. No. Did you say something dumb? Sorry. It's just that with her you have foot-in-mouth disease. I can say that because I have the same problem with Jake."

He chuckled. "I care about her but I think it's best. She's in a rush to get married and have kids. And I want those things someday, but not when I'm working seventeen-hour days like I am now."

"Well, I'm sorry. Breakups are always rough. But you're still coming to the dance, right? Jake is on duty tonight, and I need a dance partner."

"I'll be there with my boots on, literally."

We hung up and I noticed the clock.

After feeding George, I ran upstairs to shower. I'd planned to wear a dress, but then I'd found this beautiful red suit in Round Top, which was cut in a tuxedo style. It hid a multitude of sins, which is always my favorite kind of clothing.

I put on a little extra makeup because it makes me feel good. I spritzed my curls so they wouldn't be frizzy, and that was it.

"What do you think, George?" He was asleep on the couch. He grunted without opening his eyes.

"I'm going to take that as *you look awesome, Ainsley.*"

Before I left, I made a quick call to Jasmine's new office assistant, Lavinia.

"Ms. Levy's office, how may I direct your call?"

"This is Investigator McGregor. I'm following up on some cases and have a couple of questions for you."

There was a long pause. Maybe she recognized my voice or didn't buy my investigator title. But I was investigating, so it wasn't a lie.

"I don't think I'm allowed to speak to anyone without

one of the lawyers present. No one in the company is."

"It's an investigation—you don't need permission. And it's two simple questions."

"I—Okay. What do you need to know?"

"Was Nia Levy acting strangely at all?"

"I don't know what you mean."

"Was she coherent in the weeks before her death or did she act out of character?"

"No. I mean, she was in a bit of mood but that made sense. Mr. Levy was very ill and she was trying to help Mr. Leon run the company. But she seemed fine."

That did not jive with what the sisters had said.

"And she left around noon; do you know where she went?"

"I'm sorry, I don't. The police asked me a couple of times. It was unusual, as I put her daily schedule together. But she canceled everything. She said she had family business. I thought she might need to be with her sisters and to grieve in private."

"One more question: what was her relationship with her father like?"

"Um."

"Yes?"

"They got along for the most part. There was a mutual respect. He was pretty hard on her but she had a great sense of humor. She called him old man, but it was like a joke. And I know she was worried about him when he became ill."

That didn't sound like the contentious relationship I'd expected.

I hung up, and made some notes real quick.

About twenty minutes later, I dropped George off at the daycare, or night care in this case. Community events in Sweet River always tried to provide childcare, so that parents and the kids could have fun. Maria and Carrie had volunteered to look after the little people, and of course, George, who is something of a celebrity among the kindergarten set.

It's never fun to walk into a party alone, but I didn't really have a choice. I perused the auction items, so I'd have a good idea of what I'd be talking about later. I'm not sure why the party committee thought I'd be a good auctioneer, but I always like to do my part.

"You look gorgeous," Jasmine said.

I turned to find her in an emerald dress, and heels that would have killed me but she was supermodel gorgeous.

"I'm so glad you are here."

"I was going to head home, and then sweet Mrs. Carmichael said for me to have everything shipped here, so I don't have to go back and forth.

"She's been helping me today. She told me I had to come tonight. It doesn't feel right being at a party, when I'm still in mourning—but it's for a good cause."

"If I wasn't their auctioneer, I'd be home in my unicorn pajamas. Now that you're here, I'm glad I came. Let's go get some punch. Oh, there's your uncle and your cousin."

Her uncle wore a dark blue suit that complemented his lean frame. Her cousin Angie was dressed in a bright yellow dress that hugged her curves, and shoes to match.

"I hope you don't mind that I invited them," Jasmine said. "We're going over some business things tomorrow, so I asked them to come up. It's just easier to do things here away from the reporters. At least here, I can get out and walk around. I can't do that at home right now."

"It's crazy how much your life has changed overnight. How are you doing?"

She smiled. "It's too surreal right now for me to wrap my head around it. After years of therapy, I find out my dad loved me. Then he left the thing he loved most, his business, to me. But I'm just taking it day by day. And my therapist is on call twenty-four seven. She gets it and she gets me. That's helped me a lot."

I laughed. "I would need the same kind of help."

"These two have made everything a lot easier though." She hugged her uncle and cousin in a big group hug.

"Awwww," Angie said. "We got your back, beautiful."

"I'm so happy you two are here," I said. "It's quaint, I know. But it will give you a taste of small-town living and it's all for a good cause. The money we raise helps provide services for children and the elderly in our community."

"It's all very charming," Jasmine said. "I'm glad you invited me."

I loved that this new multi-billionaire could appreciate our small town. It spoke to the kind of person she was, and why we had such an instant kinship.

The big community hall had been decorated with twinkling lights, and red, white, and silver hearts everywhere. There were different booths along the walls with fun vignettes to take selfies. And an old-fashioned board where singles were partnered with other singles based on a random card game. Each of the singles drew a different color-coded card, and they had to find the person who had the matching one. Then, after the dance, they turned it in to get new ones. It was Sweet River's answer to the old dance card.

We'd not gotten more than a few feet, when Kane walked up.

I hadn't told Jasmine what we'd figured out because I wanted to wait. She didn't need to know at the moment that her sister killed her father, or that she might have been planning to kill Jasmine.

"Hi, Ainsley and Jasmine."

"You clean up nice," I said. "Though, you always look good."

He gave a megawatt smile, and I swear I heard Jasmine and Angie sigh. "Jasmine, I believe you're my next dance partner." He held up a light blue card, which matched the one in her hand.

"Oh. I didn't know you were single." She gave me a pointed look.

I shrugged. I didn't know until an hour ago that he'd broken up with Eva.

"I am. Would you care to dance?"

"Yes, I would." Jasmine gave him a gorgeous smile. "Thank you for taking such good care of me the other day."

I'd forgotten he'd been there when they'd done the blood tests.

"It was my pleasure." Kane gallantly held out his hand.

They did make a beautiful couple.

"Where do I sign up for that?" Angie asked.

I turned to face her. "What happened to your dad?"

"He's looking at the auction table. Seriously, where are the cards?" I pointed to a booth at the far end of the hall.

"You can have them put your name on the board."

"Love it. Bye." Angie took off as fast as her heels would allow.

"Wait," I said. "Were you close to Nia?"

She shrugged. "We hung out sometimes. The last couple of years she's been working closely with my dad. So we saw each other every once in a while."

She was glancing over my shoulder, probably in a hurry to find a man on the dating board. "Did you happen to see her the week she died?"

Angie blinked and then frowned. "Why are you giving me the third degree about Nia?"

"I'm not. It's just some of the witnesses said she'd been acting strangely. I was wondering if you'd noticed anything like that."

"No. She was kind of a serious person. Everything with her was about the business. She didn't have a lot of hobbies if you know what I mean. I tried to get her to go out and party with me and Kiara, but she never would."

"Kiara?" I played dumb.

"The youngest sister. She and I have always been great friends. She's the only one who didn't judge me when I made some mistakes back in the day."

"Okay, thank you. Go have some fun. The men in Sweet River tend to be on the handsome side."

"I've noticed," she said. "Bye. If you see my dad—just tell him I'm dancing."

I stood there going over what she'd said. The sisters had to be lying about Nia's behavior. The assistant and Angie said she'd been fine. But that didn't explain Jasmine's hallucinations when she stayed at the house. Argh. This was so frustrating.

Wait, Angie never answered my question about if she'd seen Nia the week she died.

"Should we ship them as JasKa or KaJas," Shannon said from behind me.

I glanced out on the dance floor to see Jasmine and Kane talking to one another. I started giggling. "Right? Idris and Halle dancing at the Sweet River Valentine's dance—who would of thought?"

"Where's Mike?"

"He's bidding on stuff at the silent auction. I'm not allowed to look for some reason."

"I have a feeling he's trying to snag some sort of wedding present for you guys."

"Possibly. And I wish Jake was here to see you in that suit. You are gorgeous."

I smiled. "Thanks. And I'm surprised you and Mike made it here with you in that dress."

She cleared her throat. "Might be why we were a little late." She threw a hand over her mouth. "I can't believe I sad that out loud."

We both started laughing.

"What did I miss?" Jake's voice said into my ear. I may have jumped and squeaked. Poor guy. I was going to give him a complex.

"I thought you were working?" I hugged him, and he kissed my cheek.

"I am," he said. "I'm the fire marshal for tonight. Jim called in sick."

"Oh, that's the best news I've had in forever. Not that Jim is sick, I mean. But that you're here."

"I'm on my break and I decided to ask my girl to dance."

Happy tingles soared through my body. I'm a woman, and I'm strong, but when a man calls me his girl—I like it. Or at least, when that man is Jake.

"I'd love to."

He pulled me into his arms. The slow song meant we could basically just stand there and sway. I put my arms around his neck, and his went around my waist.

"You're gorgeous," he said, and then smiled. "Though, you're always beautiful to me whether you're in unicorn pj's or a sexy suit."

I sighed happily. "You don't look awful in your uniform, either. Just sayin'."

He chuckled. I had that weird feeling that someone was watching me. I glanced over his shoulder, but didn't see anyone. I shivered.

"Are you cold?"

"No. I'm good. This was the best surprise," I said.

"I think, I might have something better." He gently drew me off the dance floor and into a shadowy corner.

Um. I wasn't big on PDA, but if Jake wanted to kiss me at the Valentine's dance, who was I to argue?

"This is for you." He reached into his pocket, and I held my breath. Was it an engagement ring? How did I feel about that? The answer came easily, I'd love it.

Wow. I didn't think I desired the whole marriage thing. But when it came to Jake, I had to throw out my old views on relationships. With Jake, I wanted everything.

The velvet box, though, wasn't ring-sized. It was much longer and from James Avery, one of my favorite jewelry designers.

"Jake, you didn't have to get me anything."

"I want you to know how special you are to me."

For a man who wasn't always great at communicating his feelings, he was doing a great job tonight.

"I feel bad. I would have brought your gift."

"Ainsley."

"Yes."

"Open your present." He gave me one of those devastating smiles.

"Yes, sir." I took the box from him, and opened it.

I gasped. Inside, was a charm bracelet. The charms were of a Great Dane, a fireman, the word *love*, and the logo for Bless Your Art. He'd had to have had that last one custom-made.

Tears sprang to my eyes. "I love it, Jake. It's perfect."

He took it out of the box and wrapped it around my wrist. It was gold, and expensive-looking. "I love you, Ainsley. I know I could say it more. But my hope is that every time you see this bracelet, you'll know how much you're loved by me, this town, and of course, George."

At that point, I may have blubbered. Okay, I did. But so he couldn't see me ugly-cry, I threw my arms around his neck and held on tight—at least, until I could get myself under control.

"It's the best gift anyone has ever given me. And I love you, too."

Then he kissed me, right there in front of half the town.

For the first time in my life, I didn't give one wit about PDA.

He pulled away, and brushed his thumb across my cheek. "I have to work. We're required to do a head count every half hour, but I'll be back for another dance."

He went off to do his fireman stuff, and Shannon and Jasmine tottered over in their heels. "What is it?" Shannon asked. "And next time, don't block our view. We couldn't see anything except the way he was looking at you."

"It's a good thing he's a fireman," Jasmine said. "Because that look he gave you was smokin' hot." She fanned her face.

I held up the bracelet for them to see.

"It's gorgeous," Jasmine said.

"He put so much thought into this, I might cry," Shannon said. "Speaking of which, here." She dug into her tiny bag and gave me a tissue. "You have a little mascara under your eyes."

"Please tell me I don't look gross," I said.

"You don't," Shannon replied. "You just have little smudges. Here, give me the tissue."

"I just have one question," Jasmine said.

"What?" I asked.

"Who is that woman over there? And why does she look like she wants to kill you?"

Chapter Nineteen

SHANNON AND I turned at the same time to see the woman Jasmine was talking about, but she was walking away at a fast pace.

"Do you know who she is?" Shannon asked.

I shook my head. "It might be that woman from the store."

"What woman?" Jasmine asked.

"I don't know her name. The day we first met, she showed up at the store. She walked up to the counter and just stared at me. Then she said, 'I don't see it.' Or something like that. And walked out of the store."

"Weird. Why didn't you tell me?" Shannon asked.

"And rude," Jasmine said. She snapped her fingers. "Do you think maybe she's one of your man's exes? He's pretty smitten with you, but he's a handsome guy. There has to be a trail of exes."

Could she be right? "I hope you're wrong. He's dated a lot of women in this town."

"Yes, but you're the one who took him off the market," Shannon said.

"Well, if you see her again, don't be shy about taking her picture. Then I can run it by Jake to see. I mean, it's a bit of stretch, but it's the only thing that makes sense. I feel…so special, I have a stalker."

We all laughed.

But I wasn't happy. Was she the one who tried to break in my house? That would be taking jealousy a little too far.

You don't even know if she's upset about Jake.

But my spidey senses tingled. That meant I was on the right path.

"If you'll excuse me, I think I'll try to find her."

"Not by yourself," Shannon said. "You need backup."

I laughed. "You don't even know it was me she was looking at."

"No, it was definitely you," Jasmine said. "I'm a little paranoid these days so I keep an eye on my surroundings, no matter where I am. She watched you and Jake over in that corner like a hawk, and she was not happy. And Shannon is right. We're coming with you."

It didn't look like I had a choice, so we pushed through the crowd of people toward the door where the woman had exited. But when we made it to the hallway, it was empty.

"The restrooms are down that way. Let's check in there," Shannon said.

That's where we found the woman from the shop. She dabbed her eyes and nose with a tissue as if she'd been crying.

When she saw us, she stuffed the tissue in her bag, and tried to get past us.

"Excuse, me," she said through gritted teeth.

"Are you upset with me about something?" I asked.

Shannon and Jasmine crossed their arms and spread their feet like some kind of Charlie's Angels security force. If I hadn't been nervous, I might have laughed.

The woman was tall and looked strong. I was pretty sure she could take all three of us, easily. Especially, since none of us knew how to fight.

"It's none of your business," she said. "Get out of my way or I'm calling the police."

"Oh, please do," I said. "The sheriff is my brother and I bet he'd be interested to know why you were trying to break into my house the other night. I sure would."

Her eyes went wide and to the left.

Got you.

It was her.

Shannon and Jasmine glanced at each other, and Shannon pulled out her phone and started texting someone.

"I saw you," I said. Liar. But I had to get to the bottom of this.

Her blond hair was in a ponytail and she wore dark jeans, a red top and red cowboy boots.

"I wasn't trying to break in," she said. "I was just going to leave you a note but I thought your dog was coming through the door. No guy is worth losing a limb."

"What guy? Jake?"

"Yes. I met him when we were training a few months ago."

Wait, was that why Jake had been so weird when he'd been away? "So, you guys dated?"

"We spent time together. He wasn't intimidated by my strength and commitment to my job, like the other guys. We had fun together."

A knot formed in the pit of my stomach. This feeling

was why I never did relationships. And why I had trust issues.

But Jake's a really good guy. I tried really hard to think about that.

"She's lying, Ains," Shannon said. "She's just trying to get you worked up. Jake wouldn't cheat on you."

"We weren't really dating, yet," I said. "But he told me he barely had time to breathe. So, I'm wondering how you were able to date?"

"Close quarters. His room was right next to mine."

Ugh. Bile rose in my throat.

"That was months ago, so why are you here?"

"I was living in El Paso, but I just moved to Austin, which is closer. I thought he and I could pick up where we left off. But he said he was in a relationship with you.

"That day I came to your shop, I'd just been to see Jake. It was my first time to ever ask a guy out. But he told me he was serious about you and that it was a long-term commitment. Like the forever kind."

I might have done a silent yay, internally.

"So, why didn't you go home?" Jasmine said.

"I don't give up that easily." She narrowed her eyes. Oh. My. That was scary.

But I would not cower to this woman. I straightened my shoulders. "No one is more surprised than I am that Jake is in love with me."

"Obviously, you haven't seen you in that pantsuit," Shannon said. I'm sure she was trying to use humor to defuse the situation. The woman had problems, ones that might be dangerous.

"Wait, did you cut the battery cable?" Shannon asked.

The woman nodded and stared menacingly at me. "I'm good at setting fires."

Had she meant to burn down the building with us in it?

Jasmine cleared her throat. "You wanted to kill us."

"I'm not a murderer," the woman said. "But I heard you talking about your wedding the other night, and I figured if the place wasn't there then you couldn't get married. That would give me time to convince Jake that he had it wrong."

Yep. Definitely something wrong with her.

"It would have been my wedding you'd have destroyed," Shannon said in a dark voice. I'd never heard her that way. "I'm the one getting married." She growled.

For the first time, the woman blanched.

Shannon stepped forward, and I put an arm out to stop her.

Someone banged on the door. "Police!"

We all stood staring at one another.

"Ainsley, are you in there?" my brother shouted.

Before I could answer, the door slammed open and whacked Shannon. She twirled, and slipped. Jasmine tried to catch her, and they both ended up in a pile on the floor.

"Look what you did!" I shouted.

"What is going on!" Greg shouted back. "Are you okay? Shannon texted 911 for this location."

"Is Ainsley in there?" That was Jake. "Is she okay?"

These are my monkeys and this is my circus.

"Everyone stop shouting," I said. "No one is hurt, except for Shannon. I'm pretty sure you just busted her face," I said. "I hope you have EMTs standing by. Jake, your girlfriend is in here."

"I know, Ainsley, I'm talking to you."

I don't know why but I started laughing hysterically. Jasmine and Shannon joined me.

Greg stared at us, as if we were one giant conundrum.

Jake pushed past him and took in the scene. "Jenny, what the heck are you doing here? Did you hurt Ainsley?" His voice grew rough and he pushed me behind him.

"I'm okay," I said.

"Jenny, answer my question. Why are you here?"

"To tell her the truth. That you and I are meant to be together."

"I told you to go home. I was nice to you, Jenny. That was it. I could see the other guys were giving you a hard time. If you thought something else, you're wrong."

"You can lie all you want," Jenny said. "But your girlfriend knows the truth. Let's see how long she sticks around now."

Ahhhh. There it was. She wanted to scare me into giving up Jake.

Shannon was right—she'd been lying. Jake was a great guy, and his morals were above reproach.

"Oh, I'm here for the long haul," I said. "I'm not going anywhere. You, however, will be heading to jail. She's the one who cut the battery cable and she'd planned on burning down the Old Barn when we were in it."

"What?" Jake and Greg yelled at the same time.

"You can't prove any of that."

Jasmine held up her phone. "She can. I have you admitting to everything on my recorder."

Jenny jumped forward to grab the phone, but Greg caught her by the arm, and shoved her against one of the stalls.

"That's enough," he said loudly. "You're under arrest…"

"Jake, take poor Shannon and pray Greg hasn't broken her nose. Her wedding is next week."

Shannon whimpered in the corner. I was so worried about that. She might never forgive me if I ruined her wedding photos.

Jake turned and hugged me. "Ainsley, I love you. I have pretty much since the day we first met and I haven't looked at another woman. She's been telling you lies."

I smiled. "I know."

The shock on his face was priceless. "You do?"

"I nodded. You're nice to everyone and treat them equally. She just misconstrued the situation."

He hugged me tight and then pulled me into the hallway. "God, if she'd hurt you, I'd never have forgiven myself."

Mike was running down the hall looking like he was ready to go into battle.

"What's going on?" he roared. "I just saw Shannon's text."

"Everything is fine. Though she had an incident with the door. Jake, please get everyone out of here. We need to get the EMTs to take a look at Shannon."

"Babe?" Mike shouted.

"I'm okay," Shannon said. "I think."

"Ms. Levy, I'll need your phone—if you could drop it by the station later," Greg said. "And I'm going to need all three of you to make statements," Greg said, then he led Jenny down the hall.

When Shannon came out of the stall, her face devoid of any injuries, I was shocked.

"Thank goodness they didn't hit your face." Relief poured through me. This was my drama and I didn't want it to ruin her day.

"Jasmine was trying to pull me out of the way when Greg busted through the door. Thank goodness." But she held a wad of paper towels on top of her head.

"Oh, that doesn't look good," I said.

"There's a lot of blood but that happens with head wounds," Jake said.

"She's got a goose egg and a small gash, which will probably need stitches," Jasmine added.

Shannon paled, but before she could pass out, she was in Mike's big, beefy arms. "I got you, babe."

Just then a crowd started down the hallway. It was the gang from the shop with Mrs. Whedon leading the pack, doing her fast job.

"Is there trouble? What did you do now, Ainsley?" Mrs. Whedon asked.

"Ainsley had a stalker or Jake did," Shannon offered.

There were gasps all around as they saw all the blood. It looked very dramatic.

"Are you girls okay? We came ready to fight." Mrs. Whedon held up her umbrella.

I started laughing. I couldn't stop.

"Mike, why don't you take Shannon to the truck," Jake said in his best authoritative voice. He was determined to get the situation under control. I liked that about him. "We'll figure out if she needs to go to the hospital."

That sobered me up fast. I cleared my throat. "Will one of you do the auction for me? I need to give my statement to the police." I stared pointedly at Mrs. Whedon. She was great at holding an audience captive. I'd seen her do it more than once.

"I'll take care of it," she said. "Are you sure you're okay?" She gave me that grandmotherly once-over. She'd appointed herself my guardian at Christmas. And no, I didn't ask. But I loved her.

"Yes, ma'am."

Don came huffing down the hall. Poor Santa Claus was out of breath.

He tried to talk but ended up with his hands on his knees.

"Everyone is okay," I said.

He just nodded.

"Come on, let's go check on Shannon," Jake said. Then he led Jasmine and me down the hall.

"I'm not sure I could have been as levelheaded as you were," Jasmine said.

"There was something about her that scared me a little," I said. "I just wanted to keep her calm. You could have run out at any time, you know."

"Girlfriends never leave anyone behind." She gave me a side smile. "Like Shannon said, we've got your back."

"And I've got yours."

A twist of guilt gnarled itself in my stomach. But there was no way I'd tell her about her sister possibly killing their father.

At least, not until I had more facts.

Chapter Twenty

A FEW DAYS later, I was restocking the table up front with Jasmine's candles. She, her uncle and cousin were still staying at the B&B. She'd rented an office space on top of the bank building, which had the best internet in town. I hadn't really seen her much, other than when she delivered candles. The new job was taking up all of her time.

I'd been on nonstop wedding duties for Shannon. As promised, everything was organized to the letter. But each day I had certain things to check off.

Thanks to my brother, she'd taken a pretty good hit to the head, and they'd had to shave a little bit of her hair off to stitch her up.

Luckily, thanks to her veil, her head would be covered up. And we'd found a cute little hat she could wear during the reception. I was trying to figure out which candles to stack next, when Kane walked in.

"I'm in a rush," he said. "But I wanted to let you know the police think you might be right about two killers. The catch is they are no closer to figuring out who murdered Nia."

"I'm glad you guys listened. But can I ask why they agree?"

"You pointed it out early on. Poison is personal. But it's

also not the easiest thing to do right. If we could only figure out where she was before she died."

I'd given Greg the news that she'd had lunch with her uncle. I tried to think of a way that I could perhaps talk to Leon alone.

"Hmmm. Well, thanks for letting me know. Will I see you at the wedding this weekend?"

"Wouldn't miss it," he said. "Tell Shannon I said hello."

"I will."

"And, um…"

"What?"

"You can tell Jasmine hello. I mean, if you see her."

I laughed.

Well, it didn't take him long to move on.

"Hey, what are you doing here?" Mrs. Whedon asked. "You're supposed to be off the rest of the week helping Shannon."

I laughed. "It's nice to see you too, Gran." If my favorite curmudgeon wanted me to call her Gran, I would.

"Pish-posh. We can survive without you for a few days, Ainsley. I don't want you wearing yourself too thin. That's why you're always getting the sniffles. You don't get enough rest."

Obviously, she hadn't seen me on a Netflix or Hulu binge. Or that one weekend with *The Mandalorian*. I don't think Jake and I left the couch for anything more than food and bathroom breaks.

Hidden behind her gruff nature, she cared about me.

"I just came by to pick up some candles for my house," I said. "And I noticed the stock was low."

"All right but we can take care of that. Just get what you need and move along. Oh, wait, that bracelet is gorgeous." She took my hand in hers and then held up my wrist to the light. "I see," she said. "That is quality gold."

She had a smile like she knew something I didn't. "I take it, this is from Jake?"

"Yes, ma'am."

"That's a good one, Ainsley. Don't muck it up."

I laughed. "Well, he hasn't run away yet, and goodness knows I've tried."

"Yep. When you find the right one, they stick around. I'm glad he's courting you properly."

I wanted to say that it wasn't the early nineteenth century, but I held my tongue.

"Now, you go along. We've got this covered and I don't want to see you back here—understand? You deserve a little fun after the past few months."

I hugged her, and she gave me the Whedon three-tap pat on the back. After gathering up my candles, I headed back to the office. George was there, snoring so loud some of the boxes on a shelf rattled.

"Hate to wake you from your nap, buddy, but it's time to go home." I had to clean my house and get it ready for Shannon to come stay with me. Her family had taken over her apartment and most of the B&Bs in town. There were even some of them at Mrs. Carmichael's.

Mike's family was out at the winery in the big farmhouse. Originally, Shannon's cousins were going to stay at my house, but her family was driving her kind of crazy, and she'd switched things around so she could stay with me.

I had to use treats to get George to follow me out to the car.

As I drove past Mrs. Carmichael's B&B, Jasmine's sisters were getting out of a large, black SUV.

"I wonder what they're doing here?"

Jasmine had mentioned that they still weren't too happy with her, even though she had nothing to do with her father's decision.

The sisters were arguing with one another, and I didn't need my windows to be rolled down to know that.

Worried about Jasmine, I pulled over into one of the slots in front of the B&B. She had my back the other night, and I'd have hers. If nothing else, I could sit in Mrs. Carmichael's kitchen as moral support.

As I coerced George out of the car with the promise of peanut butter cookies, my mind ran through all the facts.

The sisters were out in the yard, still arguing over something.

What if all the sisters were in it together?

My heartbeat increased. If that was the case, Jasmine might really be in serious danger.

I texted her: *Don't drink or eat anything.*

She sent back a: *?*

Trust me. I need twenty minutes.

Okay.

Then I drove straight to the police station.

KEVIN WAS AT the front desk. He didn't look away from his

computer, which meant he was probably playing Fortnite again. My brother would have his head.

"Is my brother in?"

He jumped and nearly fell out of his chair. "No. He's on his lunch."

Crud.

"Is Lucy here?"

"She's back in the file room," he said, and then stared at his computer again. "Awww, man."

"Don't let me interrupt your game," I whispered as I walked by.

Lucy was sitting at a long table in the file room going through several folders.

She glanced up when I walked in.

"Sorry, I didn't want to disturb you."

"It's okay. I feel like I'm going cross-eyed," she said. "What's up?"

"I was wondering something about Nia's case," I said. "It's an idea I have that might help us figure out where she went that day."

"I'm interested. What do you want to know?"

"Her car's GPS. The sisters said she came home and changed clothes," I said. "But where did she go after that?"

"They ended up towing the car to Houston, but I should have that info somewhere in the files." She waved a hand across the table.

"Can I help? It's kind of a timing thing."

She sighed. "Why do I have the feeling you're up to something?"

"I'll explain everything, I promise—before I do the

dumb thing I'm thinking about."

She snorted. "One condition."

"What is it?"

"That I come on the dumb mission?"

It wouldn't be such a bad thing to have an officer backing me up. I had no idea what would happen once I started poking the bears.

"Deal."

For ten minutes we went through files.

"Found it," Lucy said. "We actually checked everyone's GPS that day."

She opened the file, and I walked behind her.

"Here's the one for Nia's car," she said.

"What's that address? The one before she came here?"

Lucy turned and typed something into her computer. "It's a residence. Corporate housing for executives. But it doesn't say who owns it. Let me see if I can figure it out."

"We don't have time. I need to be there while I have them all in one place," I said.

"Who?" she asked.

"The whole family is at Mrs. Carmichael's B&B. I feel like if I do one of those Agatha Christie things with everyone in the same room that one of them will break."

"No," Lucy said. "You can't do that. First, you aren't a professional. Second, it's dangerous. If you're right, there's a killer in the room with you. One who will be feeling desperate."

"Can we pretend that I didn't tell you?"

Lucy's eyebrow rose. "Your brother would say the same thing."

"Which is why I never would tell him, until I was actually doing it. But I trusted you to understand. You can just say you were suspicious of what I was about to do, so you followed me. I will never tell him that we had this conversation."

"You're going to do this no matter what I say, aren't you?"

"Well, yes."

"Do you have an idea who you're targeting?"

I nodded. "I think it's either Ebony and Lila. Or it's the uncle. Kiara may be in on it with her sisters, but she seemed the one who was most upset over Nia, and she was the happiest to see Jasmine. You can't fake the joy she had when she hugged her sister. I can't see her wanting to kill anyone."

"But you've been wrong before."

I sighed. "I'm sure you guys aren't always right. Look, you're just as frustrated with this case as I am. You'll be there and I'll be safe. And the worst that might happen is we have some awkward conversations.

"If you want, you can feed me questions. I'm totally open to do this. But something in my gut says I need to do it right now."

She frowned. "Okay. Let's do it. But I'm calling your brother as soon as you begin."

"That's fine by me."

Nerves churned in my stomach. This was a big swing and there was a good chance I'd miss.

But Jasmine might have been in danger and I was going to do whatever it took to make sure my new friend was safe.

You can do this.

Maybe.

Chapter Twenty-One

A SHORT TIME later, I was in the front parlor of the B&B with Jasmine's family. We were having tea and cookies that Mrs. Carmichael had prepared, but I wasn't eating. Jasmine was also avoiding the drinks and food.

Frogs climbed into my throat, and my stomach churned. I'd never done anything like this before.

I had that tingling feeling, though, the one that said I was heading in the right direction.

"What was it you wanted to talk to us about?" Jasmine smiled at me. I'd been worried that she might be angry with me for butting in on family time, but she'd been happy to see me and gave me a tight hug.

"Well, as you know I'm helping out with your sister's case. I do that sometimes on a consulting basis."

I swear I heard a cough, covering a laugh from somewhere near the kitchen.

"We've said everything we need to the *actual* police."

"Don't be rude, Ebony," Jasmine said. "I told you all, I don't know what I would have done without Ainsley. She's been a godsend. And she's a bit of a local legend around here when it comes to solving cases."

I wouldn't say legend, exactly. Maybe a nosy busybody, which is what my brother would say.

"It's more of a liaison thing," I said. "People don't always like talking to the police. I just try to help straighten out facts. I'd been meaning to call and check up, but a friend of mine has me busy with wedding stuff. When I drove by and saw y'all, it seemed like a good time to get your opinions and some facts."

All of that was true.

The incredulity in the room was palpable. But they didn't say anything.

This was a dumb plan.

But I was already there, so I decided to charge on.

"Right, so the police have different stories about the timeline regarding Nia the night she showed up here. Since I have you here together, I thought maybe we could get that sorted."

The people who knew her best were in one room, but this wasn't so much about trying to get a confession, as it was to see how they interacted with one another.

They all stared at me like I had three heads, but I just kept going.

"We know when she left the office early. She arrived here in town around eight forty-five. What the police are trying to piece together is where she was in between that time, and why she came here, of all places."

I was carefully watching all of them to see if there was a clue. But the faces around me were blank.

Okay.

"So, did anyone see her come home after work?"

Lila, Kiara, and Ebony glanced at one another.

Something was going on.

"Lila? You look like you have something to say."

She didn't, but I had to start somewhere.

"I. Uh—"

"We all saw her that afternoon," Ebony said. "She was acting weird. We called her on it and started fighting. She hadn't taken Dad's death well, and we were worried about her."

The lack of sincerity was obvious.

"Well, some of us were worried," Kiara said. Her eyebrow went up, which meant she wasn't happy with her sister. "Others might have been more worried about when they were going to get their inheritance."

Oh. My. Ebony's death stare was a little scary.

"Was there a confrontation?"

"Not really," Kiara said. "We were trying to talk to her through the door. She said she had a lunch to get to and that she'd talk to us later." Her face fell. "But there wasn't a later." A tear slid down her cheek, and she rubbed it away with her fingers.

"We all said things we regret that afternoon," Lila chimed in. "Ebony was furious that they hadn't read the will yet. And Kiara and I thought that Nia should be home with us, so we could all mourn together. I called her, selfish. It's the last thing I said to her."

Funny, how all the fingers seemed to point to Ebony, and she sat there stewing.

"And what did Nia say?"

"She came out dressed for her lunch, and slammed the bedroom door. All she said was that she hoped we all got what we deserved," Kiara said. "When I asked her what she meant, she said Karma wasn't on our side. We had no idea what she was talking about. I mean, none of us are angels, but she was truly angry. Like…we'd done something to her."

What if Nia hadn't been the one to kill her father? The thought hit me like a baseball bat to the head. Everyone had believed, because the tea was found in her room, that she was the guilty one.

But maybe she'd figured out one of her sisters had killed the father.

"What do you think she meant by that?"

The sisters shrugged in unison.

"If you know something that will help, please tell us," Jasmine said. "Even if you weren't happy with Nia, she didn't deserve to die like that."

"We didn't kill her," Ebony shouted. "And I'm not going to sit and listen to this. Jasmine, we only came here to convince you to come home. It's time the family was together. But if you're going to believe this pretend cop, then we have nothing left to say."

Jasmine held up both hands in a stop motion. "For the record, we're all together right now. And I like the idea of sussing this out. Maybe we can figure something that will help the police catch the killer.

"And I didn't say you did anything wrong. I just want to know why she was upset with you?"

"Tell her," Lila said to Ebony. "Maybe we can figure out what happened to our sister if everyone is honest for a change."

Ebony's facial expression was not a happy one and then she closed her eyes. She took a deep breath and seemed calmer.

"We thought she might be suffering from the same sort of mental illness Dad did," Ebony said.

There were gasps around the room. This was news to Jasmine, the uncle and Angie.

"The erratic behavior, the anger. She always seemed to be mad since Dad became ill. I mean, she was the more serious one, but she was vicious and accusatory," Ebony said. "It wasn't like her. When Jasmine left, Nia took over. She was the mother-hen type. But the last few months—she was so unhappy and it was more than just Dad being sick and her taking on more work." She waved a hand to Lila.

"We tried to talk to her about it the day after Dad died," Lila added. "But she was so unfocused and just weird. She'd say strange things. Dad did that for the last month or so. We thought it was just old-timer's disease. But when Nia started acting weird, we weren't sure what to think."

This was the first time I'd heard about any mental illness. Wait, except for the hallucinations that Jasmine had experienced. Kane said there wasn't any cyanide in Nia's system. That's why we thought Nia had done it.

"Ebony tried to get her to stay home and rest the night she died, but Nia was paranoid," Kiara added. "She said she couldn't trust anyone, least of all us."

Because one of you had tried to kill her.

"What you're saying makes sense," I said calmly, even though I was worried I sat in a room with a bunch of murderers. "I'm sure that was very disturbing for all of you."

They nodded, once again in unison. Talk about weird.

"None of you have any idea who she met for lunch that

afternoon? The police are tracking her movements through security cameras around the city, but it's taking them some time to get through all the footage."

Liar. I mean, maybe that was happening, I had no idea. But we knew exactly where Nia had gone the night she died.

I was so focused on the sisters, that I hadn't really been looking at anyone else. But then a certain someone flinched when I mentioned the cameras. Her eyes went wide.

And it was the last person on my suspect list.

Chapter Twenty-Two

I CLEARED MY throat, and then coughed twice. That was my signal to Lucy that I might have something. She was in the kitchen listening to the conversation. It was the condition. She also had a wire on me so everything would be legal.

"We told you that we had no idea where she went once she left the house."

But I had an idea.

"That's fine. Not only are they checking the cameras, but the navigation on her car will help them track her movements that day."

The suspect didn't bat an eye. Okay, maybe not that one. Bummer.

My phone buzzed and I turned it over to read the screen.

"Oh, I almost forgot. Do any of you know this address? It's the last place we believe she stopped."

Everyone shook their head, but it was Uncle Leon whose eyes stared hard at the floor.

"Are we done yet? I want to go grab something to eat," Angie said. She picked at her long nails and it was more than obvious she was bored. She yawned. "My blood sugar is dipping. Come on, Dad."

"I—Okay," he said.

Angie bustled out the door.

My phone buzzed again. It was a text from Lucy: *Address owned by Levy Corp.*

"Wait, Mr. Levy." He stopped, and even from behind, the tension in his shoulders was visible.

"I just had an update from the police. Did you know that Levy Corp owns the house at that address?"

He turned, and then cleared his throat. "We own several residences all over the world and I don't keep up with all of them."

I took a long shot. "Not even the ones you and your daughter live in?"

His shoulders jerked back as if I'd slapped him.

"Young woman, be careful where you tread. We are not answering any more of your questions."

He turned to walk out but when he opened the door, my brother stood on the other side. "Mr. Levy, you are under arrest. You have the right to remain silent."

"I didn't do it," the older man said gruffly. "This is police harassment. She's not even a real officer."

Greg ignored him and kept giving him his Miranda rights.

Everyone was talking at once.

There was something about his face that wasn't right. He didn't look like a man who was guilty. More like one who was resigned to his fate.

Something was wrong.

"Greg, wait," I said. I jumped up and the sisters stopped arguing.

"Your daughter lives in that house, doesn't she?"

"I'm not saying anything without my lawyer."

Lucy came in and I turned toward her. "We need to find Angie. I'd bet my house she's the one who did all of this. I don't know how but I'm sure of it."

"I'm going to kill her," Jasmine said.

"There's been enough of that going around," I said. "But we need to find her. She'll be feeling pretty desperate right about now, but luckily she's only been gone a few minutes."

I rushed past Greg and the uncle. And then I did the most un-Ainsley thing I've ever done: I leapt off the porch and ran for the street. Their car had to be somewhere close. I ran up and down. I had to stop in the middle of the street to catch my breath.

An engine revved and a car headed straight for me. It was like slow motion in a movie. I always think people are so dumb in the movies when they just stand there, but I was frozen.

"Ainsley, move!" Greg's voice boomed, as something hit me so hard that I went flying into the thorny holly across the street. There was an ominous crack as I hit the ground. And then I couldn't breathe.

I woke up to find Lucy on top of me. And then I burst out laughing. Well, I tried. It was more of a gasp as the air came back in my lungs.

She did the same as she rolled off me. "Are you okay?" she asked.

"Think so," I wheezed out. "I wish people would stop trying to kill me."

"Maybe don't stand in the middle of the street next time," she said.

I had scratches all over myself but I was able to stand up. I reached a hand down to help Lucy. It was the least I could do since she'd saved my life.

She tried to stand, but then started to fall when her legs gave out.

"I think I broke something," she said.

Great. I broke poor Lucy. My brother was going to kill me.

Chapter Twenty-Three

I WENT TO the hospital with Lucy, so that Greg could chase down Angie. He was obviously torn but he needed to question Leon to find out where his daughter might try to hide out.

Angie was smart enough to get away with murder; my guess is she was halfway to Mexico.

The nurses made me wait in the lobby while they checked out Lucy. She was going through X-rays and such.

"Hanging out with you is dangerous," Shannon said.

I'd been staring at the same magazine page for twenty minutes.

"Oh. Hey. What are you doing here?"

"I thought you might need some coffee and snacks."

"Let me guess, the whole town knows what happened?"

"Yep," she said, and then she sat down next to me. "So you found another killer."

She didn't sound happy.

"I did, but we let her get away. Why do you sound upset? Is something wrong? Did I forget a wedding thing?"

She rolled her eyes. "You confronted a killer without me. I feel so left out." She said it in a funny, whiny voice.

I started laughing. We were so loud people were looking at us.

"It's been a day."

"I can imagine," she said. "Any word on Lucy?"

"No. They're still examining her. The doctor is in there now. I feel terrible. I just stood there like an idiot while the car came straight toward me."

"Hey, we all know it's dangerous to hang out with you."

She laughed again and I smiled. "I used to be the only one who got hurt."

"Technically, it was your brother's fault I got hurt the other night. And you cracked the case. I'm proud of you."

Just then the sliding doors opened, and Lucy came out limping with one of those special boots on.

"Detective. Wait!" A male nurse was running after her. "You didn't sign your release papers. And I have your prescriptions."

"It's just a couple of broken toes and a twisted ankle. I don't need the meds." She signed the papers and then headed our way.

"I'm sorry," I said.

"Don't be. I've had worse."

"Well, I'm here to be chauffeur," Shannon said. "Greg was worried since your car was still at the B&B that you might need a ride. You ready to go home?"

"No. I need to get back to the station. I have to help Greg find the runner."

Just then, Jasmine ran in with Kiara right behind her. "Lucy's okay," I said.

Jasmine nodded. "That's great." Her face was strained though.

"What's wrong?" I asked.

"It's—"

"I know where she is," Kiara says. "Or at least, I have it on my phone. We used to party together all the time. For safety, we have an app so we know where the other one is. We haven't used it for years, so I forgot until just a while ago. I made the mistake of saying it out loud to my sisters and they're going after her. We have to stop them."

That was how Jake had found us the other night when we were stuck at the Old Barn.

"Let's go," Lucy said as she limped toward the door. "We're losing time."

"I guess we're going," I said.

"We're coming with you," Jasmine said.

I thought for sure Lucy might say something, but she didn't.

"She's stopped but I don't see any buildings around," Kiara said as we all jumped in the car. Lucy took shotgun, but Shannon handed me her keys.

"I'm too nervous to drive," she said. "You're better in these situations."

"Let's go, and give me your phone," she ordered Kiara.

"Yes, ma'am."

Lucy frowned. "Sorry. I get this way when I'm on the job." She glanced at the phone. "Turn right and head toward Warrenton."

That was a town not far from us, as in we had maybe a five-minute drive.

She picked up her phone. "Greg. We found her. Don't worry about it. I'm fine. Stop fussing. Listen, meet us at that new gas station in Warrenton. Yes. That one. My guess is she's ditching the car since we can track her by satellite. She's going to try and hitch a ride. I'd put it out on the radio for the truckers to steer clear. Yep. See ya in a bit."

"I'm sorry my cousin tried to kill you," Kiara said.

I wasn't sure if she was talking to me or Lucy.

"You're helping and it's not your fault," Lucy said. "See the lights up on the right? Pull in there. Stay in the car. I'm going to see if she's inside. Greg will be here any minute."

The sun was going down, but she was so pale.

"I'm coming with you," I said. "You're hurt and I'm not going to let that happen again."

"Me too," Jasmine said.

"Maybe I can talk some sense into her," Kiara said. "Right after I punch her face."

That's all we needed to break the tension.

"And I'm always in," Shannon said. "Let's go get a killer."

Lucy sighed. "Just don't do anything stupid." She glanced at me. "Like stand in the middle of the street and wait for a car to hit you."

I was going to be living with that one for a long time.

The lights inside the large gas station were garishly bright. I blinked as we walked inside. "Stay together," Lucy said. There were rows and rows of snacks and drinks.

"This place is huge," Shannon said. "Look at that candy aisle."

"We aren't here to shop," Lucy said harshly. "You three—" she pointed to Shannon, Jasmine, and me "—go that way. Do not separate. And you come with me," she said to Kiara.

"Fine, but if we find her, I get to punch her."

"Deal," Lucy said.

I had a feeling she wasn't kidding.

We went up and down the aisles. "Maybe you two should wait in the car."

"Nope," Shannon and Jasmine said together.

"You're worried she might be dangerous," Jasmine said.

"I know she is, and she's going to feel cornered. She may have poison with her, and it's extremely toxic. Just touching it could kill you."

Shannon sighed. "Sometimes being brave really sucks."

"There's no shame in going back to the car," I said.

"Not going to happen." As we rounded a corner toward automotive stuff, I saw a flash of red. The same color Angie had been wearing.

I started running toward the exit.

She was by some gas pumps that were for the big rigs.

"Angie, stop." She kept running fast in her six-inch heels. I was in my trademark Keds, and I couldn't get close.

Though I'd already done too much of that for one day, I wasn't about to let her get away.

Lights and sirens flashed all around us. The cavalry had arrived.

She stopped and turned around. "Don't come any closer!" she screamed. Her eyes were wide and her red hair was flying everywhere. "I'll kill you. You ruined everything."

"What did I ruin? Did you kill Nia?"

She took something out of her purse and held it out.

Angie stared at Jasmine. "The night she came to the house, she wanted to know if I had some idea where you were. She thought it was important to tell you about your dad, and she was determined for you to come home."

Jasmine gave her a tight smile. "Did you tell her I was here?"

"I showed her your website. I hadn't talked to you in a few weeks, but I said that you usually kept your calendar up to date."

What I'd said to Kane was right. She had found her through the website.

"Thank you," Jasmine said. "I appreciate that you sent her my way. At least I got to see her before she died. Did you mean to kill her?"

"She didn't care about you," Angie said viciously. "None of them do. I'm the only one."

"But why?" Jasmine asked. "You knew Dad and I were talking and that I planned to visit the house in a few months."

Angie wasn't aware, but there were several deputies behind her.

For the first time in several minutes, I felt like I could breathe.

"Yes, but I didn't think he'd leave you everything. My dad deserved to take over the company. He's too nice for his own good. And then Nia was talking to him about retiring. As if none of his contributions meant anything. He's the reason it succeeded, not your dad. He deserved to be the one in the power seat. He gave his life to that company."

"What are you talking about?" Jasmine asked.

"Aren't you proud, Jas? I used my chemistry degree, just like you wanted. I framed Nia for her dad's murder. Because with both of them out of the way, my dad could run the company. Finally. It would all be his."

A figure came up beside me and I turned to find Leon there.

"Angie, what have you done?" Her father had tears streaming down his face. "I love my nieces, I had to make sure their father's legacy lived on—that's why I was there for them. I never wanted to be in power. Why would you do something like this?"

Angie shrugged. "I thought Nia would drive into a tree or something," Angie said, as if she hadn't heard her father. "That was my plan. I'd ordered those mushrooms off the internet. I gave her that tea maker, and told her that special tea for her dad was from my herbalist. Well, it was. I just added something."

She was insane. Angie, the life of the party and goodtime girl, was a cold-blooded killer.

"But then she came to me that night. She said that she found a copy of your dad's will and he was giving it all to you. She wasn't even upset. Like, she was happy. She wanted to be the one to tell you."

At this point, Jasmine was sobbing. Shannon moved beside her, and helped prop her up.

"Angie, love, put down what you have in your hands. We have the best lawyers. We'll sort this out. There's no reason to hurt anyone else, or yourself."

"You don't get it, Dad. If I kill Jasmine, then it's yours."

Leon sighed wearily beside me. "I don't want it. I never did. I was the one who reached out to Nia about retiring. I wanted to make sure she felt comfortable."

Poor guy. Nothing ruined a day faster than realizing your daughter was a killer.

"What?"

Angie's hands dropped and whatever she had been holding hit the ground. We all took a step back, including her dad.

"I was retiring so we could travel the world like we'd always talked about. You're right, I was too busy working all the time. It was time for me to rest."

"No. No. No," Angie screamed. "I did all of this for you, Dad. All of it."

She was still screaming as Greg cuffed and Mirandized her.

Her dad grabbed my arm as he collapsed on the ground.

"Greg," I yelled. And then, we were surrounded. The EMTs pushed me aside.

"Come on," Lucy said. She reached down a hand to help me up. "We need to get you guys out of here."

"Don't you need statements?"

"Why? There are fifteen deputies who witnessed the confession."

"And I have it on my phone," Shannon added.

"Hey, that's my trick," Jasmine put in. She didn't look too good.

"That did not go the way I expected," I said. "I'm so sorry about this."

"Girl, we wouldn't have ever known that witch killed our daddy and sister, if it weren't for you. You got game," Kiara said. "I always thought Angie was a little off—but Lord."

"You said it sister," Lila added. She and Ebony must

have finally made up.

"I feel so bad about Nia," Ebony said. She had tears in her eyes. "She must have been scared out of her mind."

"I'm kind of scared to go home," Lila said. "Goodness knows what's been poisoned. We need to toss everything out. Maybe we should just move.

"And, Jasmine, we're here for you. Through the years, all of us have worked at the company from time to time. If you need to brainstorm, or whatever—we're here. We were coming to tell you that before all this happened."

Jasmine smiled and group-hugged her sisters.

"Well first order of business is I'm making you all board members," Jasmine said. "Going forward, we're going to make decisions together about our company. And no more secrets. Just like the old days when Momma was alive and we'd fight. We'd go to our rooms to cool down and then we'd come back and work it out. We aren't ad. We can be adults and give each other the grace to express how we feel. But we do it in private. Understood? We will not give the media anymore fodder. We've been through enough."

"Yes, ma'am," Kiara said.

"I don't know about you all, but I need some wine." Jasmine rubbed the bridge of her nose.

"Oh no. I left George at Mrs. Carmichael's. He's never going to forgive me."

"Jake picked him up when you rode with Lucy to the hospital," Shannon explained. "He's being taken care of."

"Ainsley, if it weren't for you, we might have never known the truth," Jasmine said. "What gave you the idea to get us all together like that? It worked brilliantly."

I wasn't about to tell her I got it from an episode of *Death in Paradise*—one of my favorite detective shows.

"Just came to me when I saw your sisters walking up to Mrs. Carmichael's. But I really do need to get home."

She hugged me. "Thank you, for everything. Girl, you're family. If you ever need anything, don't hesitate."

I smiled at her. "Well, when you get a chance, we need some more of your love candles. We're still running out, and the serenity ones."

She laughed. "After the stress of today, I may be up all night making candles. I'll have plenty for you."

"About that, do you think you'll have time for all of that now that you're in charge of your father's company?"

"Yes. Making candles is my form of stress relief. I like that people love them so much and that my work makes them happy."

"And?" Ebony asked.

"I have you guys to help out with the company. I'm going to set it up so that I'm checking in daily with the business. I thought that Uncle Leon would be running the day-to-day, but we'll figure it out. There's a good team in place. Dad followed his own advice about that. Surround yourself with good people.

"So in answer to your question, Ainsley, I will be making candles. And I'm even thinking about moving here."

"Really?" Ebony and I said it at the same time and then both laughed.

"After living in L.A. and Houston, I like this small-town life. It's quiet here and the people are kind."

"Oh, that just makes me happy," I said. And then I

hugged her.

"And I'll have more privacy," she said. "I don't like the feeling of being trapped in my own apartment. I just hope they don't find out where I am."

"You don't need to worry about your privacy," I said. "Well, everyone in town will know all your business, but we're protective of our own. We don't tell strangers what's happening. And I know that the local sheriff is not a fan of paparazzi, so you'll be fine."

She hugged me. "Thank you, again, for everything. And for being…"

"Nosy?"

She pointed at me. "Yes, that."

We all laughed.

"Okay. Let me know if you need anything. And I'll see you at the wedding?" Shannon asked.

"I'll be there." Jasmine gave us both another hug.

Then, arm in arm, she walked away with her sisters. They'd all been through a horrible shock, but she was back with her family.

And now that the killer had been caught. They'd be safe.

Chapter Twenty-Four

SHANNON DROPPED ME off at the B&B. She was grabbing her stuff from her apartment, and then meeting me at my house. I had to stop and buy groceries and clean before she got there.

I was exhausted and emotionally drained. But I would put on my happy face for the bride-to-be because she would do the same for me.

I stopped to get the basics: candy, cupcakes, mini marshmallows, and our favorite hot chocolate mix. Then I headed home.

But when I pulled in the drive, Jake's truck was there, along with the little Mini that Mike had given Shannon for her birthday.

"Great. They've already seen my mess."

"Hey, Ains," Shannon said as I walked in. She sat on my couch. George sat so close to the door, I couldn't open it the whole way.

"Hey," I said.

I bent down on my knees and hugged him. "I'm sorry I left you again," I said. "I bought you a special treat."

He slurped my face and then sat.

I handed him a peanut butter bone I had picked up at the store.

Jake walked in carrying a tray of baby quiches, my favorite appetizer. He had on my Kiss the Cook apron, and giant oven mitts. My heart may have sighed happily, or maybe I did it out loud.

I could get used to coming home to this.

A soft lemon scent filled my senses. I forced myself to look away from him to face Shannon. "Did you clean my house?" She has OCD and it wouldn't have been the first time. But she couldn't have beaten me by much. I'd only taken an extra twenty minutes.

The blankets were folded neatly on the couch; there wasn't a speck of dust anywhere. Even George's muddy paw prints from earlier today were gone.

"That would be your new butler." She pointed at Jake.

He smiled, as he sat down the tray on the coffee table. "Greg called and told me what happened," he said. "George, that is people food. Come on, I think I saw Mr. Squirrel on the fence."

It was unusual for my dog to turn away from food, but he understood the word squirrel. He took off so fast, he slid on the wood of my kitchen floor and almost slammed into the back door. He stopped himself before he hit the wood, and then barked at Jake.

"Dude. I'm coming." He turned back to me. "Do not say anything until I get back. I want to hear the details."

When Jake came back, he carried another tray. This one had glasses of whiskey, and another that had what looked like hot chocolate.

"I wasn't sure what kind of night it would be," he said. Then he sat down in one of the chairs across from the couch.

"Now tell me everything."

After dumping my bag on the front entry table, I grabbed one of the glasses of whiskey.

"It has been one crazy day," Shannon said. "But I'm sticking with water. I don't want my skin to break out before the wedding."

I drank several sips of the whiskey, and when it hit my shoulders, I sighed.

"How is your head?" I asked. I needed a minute to gather my thoughts.

"According to Mike, hard as a rock. It's tender but good. Now stop stalling and tell him what happened."

We live in Sweet River, and Mrs. Carmichael would have heard it all. I'd be surprised if the whole town didn't know all the details, but I told him everything.

"That was so smart of you," Shannon interjected.

"Interesting," Jake said. He smiled. "For once, you actually had an officer with you and some backup. Maybe you're learning."

"Ha-ha."

"Well, I like the old-school way of bringing all the suspects together in one room," Jake said. "It reminds me of that detective show you like. The one at the beach. And it's much safer than you climbing on top of a roof and getting shot."

"What he said." Shannon stuffed a quiche in her mouth.

"I don't want to look a gift horse in the mouth, but why did you do all of this, Jake?"

"Can't a guy just do something nice for the woman he loves?"

Shannon and I glanced at each other and started laughing.

"What?" he said.

"You either did something, or you want something," Shannon said. "And that comes from a woman who is madly in love with her man."

Jake stared down at his boots.

Oh. No more drama. I wasn't sure I could take it.

"I got an email from Jenny Anderson's captain."

"Who?" Shannon asked.

I was right there with her for a few seconds. And then I remembered. "Bathroom drama," I said.

"Ohhhhhh," Shannon said.

"And?" I asked.

"She's been formally charged. Turns out you weren't the only one who had been stalked by her. She's going to jail for a long time. But you may have to testify."

I shrugged. "If it comes to that, I will. She needs help. I think I'd like to close that chapter tight."

He got up and then came and sat by me. "Nothing happened. I need for you to believe that. I haven't been with anyone since—well, since you showed up summer before last in those denim shorts and that pink top."

"Jake!" I slapped his arm. But I had no idea he'd even noticed who I was, other than Greg's sister.

We sat there staring at one another.

"I'm going to run upstairs and change into my llama pajamas. You two have ten minutes to make out on the couch and then it's girls' night."

Jake took me in his arms.

"Ten minutes!" Shannon shouted from upstairs.

"I really am sorry she put you through all of that," he said. "But I need you to make me a promise."

"What?"

"If strange things happen around here, you tell me about it. I don't care how silly it might seem."

"I promise."

I kissed him. "I do believe you, Jake. I may have had a few minutes of doubt, but then it dawned on me, she was just making insinuations. Like that your room was next to hers, so that I would think the worst."

"It wasn't. She was separated from the rest of us. I was just being nice to her. I did nothing to lead her on."

I sighed. "I think she hasn't been around a lot of nice people. So, when she found one, she got a little too attached. But it's over. And I love you."

"I love you, more," he said and then nuzzled my neck.

"Now go, Shannon needs her Ainsley time."

He sighed. "I'm jealous. I want my Ainsley time."

After kissing me, he reluctantly got up. I followed him into the kitchen where he hung the apron up on the hook in my pantry.

"Hey, Jake?"

"Yes?"

"Anytime you want to play butler, just let me know."

He chuckled. "Promises, promises." He left.

Shannon came downstairs looking adorable in her cute pj's. She held out two pink boxes. "Do you want the gold mask or the diamond one?"

"You choose."

"Gold it is," she handed it to me. "You know what

Ains?"

"What?"

"Jake loves you so much. Like, he was cleaning house because he was worried about you. All Greg told him was that you were with the suspects and that you were safe but it was touch and go. He didn't know how long it would take. I thought he might scrub through your quartz countertop."

I scrunched up my nose. Tears burned in my eyes.

"Oh no. What did I say?" Shannon said. The poor thing was horrified.

"No. It's not that. Jake—I've just never had someone like him who worried about me."

"Like, he couldn't live without you kind of worried," Shannon said quietly.

I sighed. "Yes."

"But it's kind of awesome, right?"

"Yes. It is."

"Think you can stay out of trouble long enough to get through my wedding?" She laughed when she said it.

"I'll try," I said wearily, and then I smiled. "Let me go change, and we'll get this pre-wedding spa night going."

I let George in and he followed me.

Upstairs, as I changed, it hit me.

I hadn't been jealous about Jenny. I'd been shocked at first when she mentioned where they'd met. But I trusted Jake and I knew how he felt about me.

I stared at my dog.

"George, I think I might be emotionally mature."

He cocked head and grunted, "Rah."

I started giggling and couldn't stop.

"Nah. You're probably right."

Epilogue

I STOOD NEXT to Shannon holding her bouquet with mine. The happiness she expressed as she and Mike said their vows was contagious. I couldn't stop smiling, even though a tear slipped down my cheek.

I glanced over at Jake, who stood next to Greg, who was Mike's best man. His eyes were watery.

And that's why I love him.

As if he sensed me looking, he glanced up and smiled. And then he winked.

"You may kiss the bride," the minister said.

The joy of the moment seeped into my soul. Love was a wonderful thing when shared between two amazing human beings.

Shannon was all smiles when she turned to take her bouquet back, and then she gave me a big hug.

"You're next," she whispered.

I laughed.

She and Mike headed down the aisle. Jake took my arm in his and we followed a few feet behind them.

"They are so happy," he said.

"Yes. I'm so excited for them and today has been magical."

"It has. Someday it will be you and me walking down the

aisle," he said softly.

I tripped, but he's so strong, he kept me from face planting.

"Is that a problem?" Jake asked.

"Nope."

We both laughed.

A FEW HOURS later, as he took me in his arms, I looked out onto the dance floor. Shannon and Mike were dancing, and Kane and Jasmine were gazing into each other's eyes.

Jake touched my cheek and brought my attention back to him.

"What are you thinking?"

"Just how amazing my life is now," I said. "I have you, and the best friends in the world. I live in a place where people look out for one another. It's a life I never thought I'd have."

I laid my head on his chest.

"But it's one you deserve."

My life before Sweet River wasn't horrible. But it wasn't this.

Greg and Lucy started dancing beside us.

"Did you tell her?" Greg asked.

I pulled my head off his chest to stare at Jake.

"Tell me what?"

"Your brother and I went in on a gift for you."

I scrunched up my face and stared from Jake to my brother. "I don't feel so good." Nerves boiled in the pit of my stomach.

Lucy laughed. "Just tell her before you scare her to death."

"We signed you up and paid for a series of classes to be a private investigator."

I must have looked surprised and not in a good way.

"It's a compliment," Jake said. "Greg thinks you have real potential as a detective. But he thinks you'll be safer, if you hone your skills."

They both seemed so excited. I didn't want to mention that I owned a shop that I loved, and I taught full-time. I didn't want to solve crimes, it just sort of happened.

"Just think," Jake said. "Ainsley McGregor, Private Detective."

I smiled.

It did have a ring to it.

The End

Want more? Check out another Ainsley McGregor mystery, *A Case for the Toy Maker*!

Join Tule Publishing's newsletter for more great reads and weekly deals!

If you enjoyed *A Case for the Candle Maker*, you'll love the next book in....

The Ainsley McGregor series

Book 1: *A Case for the Winemaker*

Book 2: *A Case for the Yarn Maker*

Book 3: *A Case for the Toy Maker*

Book 4: *A Case for the Candle Maker*

Book 5: *A Case for the Cookie Baker Coming June 2021!*

Available now at your favorite online retailer!

About the Author

Bestselling and award-winning author Candace Havens has had more than thirty novels published. She is one of the nation's leading entertainment journalists and has interviewed countless celebrities from George Clooney to Chris Pratt. She does film reviews on Hawkeye in the Morning on 96.3 KSCS.

Thank you for reading

A Case for the Candle Maker

If you enjoyed this book, you can find more from all our great authors at TulePublishing.com, or from your favorite online retailer.

Made in the USA
Monee, IL
26 August 2021